because she saw desire looming in the depths of his gaze. As if he already knew what she was about to ask. As if he'd considered the very same thing.

Maybe he did know. Maybe he had.

"You're trouble," he said. "I knew it the second I saw you."

"Yeah? Well, you're trouble, too. But…I like it." *Oh!* Where had that come from? She blinked another half-dozen times, breathed again. "I might like it."

"Tell me, Goldi," he said. "If I have to guess, I might guess wrong."

It was now or never. So, *now please.*

"A kiss. I want you to kiss me."

Th

A BRIDE FOR THE MOUNTAIN MAN

BY
TRACY MADISON

First Published in Great Britain 2017
By Mills & Boon, an imprint of HarperCollins*Publishers*
1 London Bridge Street, London, SE1 9GF

© 2017 Tracy Leigh Ritts

ISBN: 978-0-263-92332-2

23-0917

Our policy is to use papers that are natural, renewable and recyclable products and made from wood grown in sustainable forests. The logging and manufacturing processes conform to the legal environmental regulations of the country of origin.

Printed and bound in Spain
by CPI, Barcelona

Tracy Madison is an award-winning author who makes her home in northwestern Ohio. As a wife and a mother, her days are filled with love, laughter and many cups of coffee. She often spends her nights awake and at the keyboard, bringing her characters to life and leading them toward their well-deserved happily-ever-afters one word at a time. Tracy loves to hear from readers. You can reach her at tracy@tracymadison.com.

Chapter One

There were many ways a person could die. Before this moment, Meredith Jensen had never given much thought to how her life might come to an end.

Why would she? She had youth, good health and a rather safe existence on her side.

Other than her penchant for over-easy eggs paired with buttered toast every Sunday morning, she didn't participate in dangerous activities. Her weekends weren't spent skydiving or bungee jumping, she drove a Volvo S60 and not a sports car and most nights, she was tucked securely into bed with a book no later than ten. As far as her career went, until two weeks ago, she'd worked as a stager for a high-end, prestigious construction and realty company in the San Francisco Bay area. Dressing up the interiors of spectacular houses, apartments and condos to make them more desirable for prospective buyers held very little risk.

And oh, how she'd loved her job.

The creativity involved, the process of designing each room around the architecture and the lighting and the scavenger hunt in locating the perfect accompaniments to bring her vision to reality. She supposed something unfortunate could have occurred if she'd been on a job-site at the wrong moment, but truly, the vast majority of her time was either spent in her office or canvassing the city in search of the right furniture, artwork, rugs and anything else she had deemed necessary.

If Meredith had spent any amount of time considering her demise, a whopper of an earthquake would've topped the list, due to where she lived. Everyday tragedies, such as car accidents, house fires and random acts of violence would have been noted, as well. To be complete, she would've included illness as an additional possibility.

But getting lost in the mountains of Colorado while the heavens unleashed a torrential, icy downpour outside her rental car? In the middle of October, no less? Nope. The predicament she currently found herself in wouldn't have landed a spot on her personal scenarios-of-death list. This trip was meant to be an opportunity to catch up with an old friend, relax, indulge in some skiing and most important…make peace with her past and reassess her future.

If everything had gone according to plan, she would have arrived at her friend Rachel Foster's house over an hour ago and would certainly be enjoying a glass of wine this very second. Naturally, Rachel had offered to pick her up from the airport, but Meredith wanted to have a car at her disposal. She had GPS, Rachel's address and her phone number. That and the Honda Accord she rented was all she needed.

Except the weather had turned on a dime shortly after

she'd left the airport, going from cold to freezing temperatures and drizzling rain to an icy mess, as if Mother Nature had flipped the "storm switch" out of boredom or anger.

She shouldn't be surprised, really. While the vast majority of Meredith's life had gone precisely according to plan, recently fate seemed determined to push her off course onto one bumpy, twisty road after another.

A small, semihysterical laugh, born from desperation and fear, escaped her. No, maybe she hadn't sensed disaster looming when she'd boarded her plane in San Francisco earlier that afternoon, but all things being considered, she should have.

Squinting her eyes in an attempt to focus on the narrow mountain road, Meredith looked for a clearing to turn the car around. Obviously, she'd gone left when she should've gone right or vice versa. Not that she had any idea of exactly where she'd erred. Because of her location, the weather or a combination of both, her phone had lost its signal thirty-plus minutes ago.

No GPS. No way to search for directions from her current location. No way to call or text Rachel or to reach out for help. She was on her own.

And didn't that feel like some type of a sick joke?

To make matters worse, as late afternoon crawled its way toward dusk, snowflakes had joined the wintry mix and now whipped through the air, their numbers seemingly multiplying by the minute. They fell hard and fast, covering the ground in a growing sheath of white. She was, as her much loved and dearly departed grandmother used to say, in quite the pretty pickle.

Meredith drew her bottom lip into her mouth and tried to hold back the panic rippling through her blood. Barely able to see through the windshield, driving as slow as she could manage in deference to the slick, icy road, she said a silent prayer for her safety. Then, right on the heels of that, she gave herself a swift, mental kick in the butt.

"Be smart," she said. "Stop feeling and start thinking. There will be plenty of time to fall apart later."

Right. Assuming she lived, she could give in to hysterics as much as she wanted once she got out of this mess. And the first step had to be reversing her direction, so she could attempt to find one of the houses she'd driven past and hope for a kind Samaritan who would be willing to take her in until the weather cleared. Locating Rachel's house at this point was akin to finding a solitary needle in a hundred—no, make that a thousand—haystacks.

Leaning forward in her seat and completely removing her foot from the gas pedal, Meredith peered through the windshield. The sky was darkening quickly, the sun's already dimming glow further diminished by clouds and snow, rain and ice.

She couldn't even see far enough in front of her to know if she was approaching a bend in the road or a cross street she could use for a U-turn. Other than her headlights, there weren't any lights to be seen, whether from oncoming cars, houses or businesses that might be tucked off the road.

The terror that Meredith had worked so hard to contain engulfed her in a rush, sending a tremor of shivers through her body.

Where the hell was she?

How had she managed to find what had to be one of the very few mountain roads in a tourist town filled with skiers that wasn't populated with residences, hotels or any other signs of human existence?

She couldn't see a damn thing, so she braked to a full stop, the tires sliding precariously on the icy road before obeying her command. With the car engaged in Park, she switched on the emergency lights—just in case she was fortunate enough for another vehicle to come along— opened the door and stepped outside.

Okay, yeah, it was cold. The type of cold that hurt.

Edging to the side of the road, she walked forward, looking for what she hadn't been able to see from the car: a wide, relatively flat and clear space she could use to turn the car around.

In mere seconds, her hands were tingling from the frigid temperature and the slashing wintry mix. She hadn't been thinking clearly. She should have grabbed her coat from the back seat before leaving the car. She didn't bother turning back. She wouldn't be out here for long.

Tugging down her sleeves to use as makeshift gloves, eyes downcast, she trudged forward. In careful, small steps, she navigated a path through the thickening snow and around the outer layer of trees—a mix of deciduous and coniferous, mainly aspen, pine, spruce and fir—that blanketed this section of the mountainside.

Earlier, before the drastic change in the weather and becoming hopelessly lost, she'd marveled at the natural beauty of these trees, of their rich and varied shades of green and gold, with splashes of red, atop a canopy of pure white leftover from a prior snowfall. Now, they were nothing more than another set of obstacles, blocking her route and her vision. Still beautiful, without doubt, but entirely unhelpful.

Her arms, legs and feet were already numb. Her cheeks already raw, her lips chapped and her hair a mass of wet, frozen strands.

She couldn't have traveled more than twenty feet from the car, but what would've been an inconsequential distance in the full light of day and under normal circumstances might as well have been two hundred miles. It was just too cold, too gray and shadowed, too windy, too…everything. Each step she took away from the car increased her brewing panic. She kept at it for a few more minutes, without any luck, before deciding she'd gone far enough.

If there was an easy spot to turn around, she couldn't see it.

Okay. No biggie. She'd just keep driving in the same direction and hope she'd come across a house, a hotel, a gas station or a restaurant. An igloo. Somewhere, anywhere, that would offer safety until the storm passed.

"Please, please let there be shelter just up the road," she whispered into the frigid air as she stumbled in retreat toward her waiting car. Somewhere with food would be a tremendous bonus, as she hadn't eaten anything that day. She never did before getting on a plane.

A burger dripping with melted cheese would taste like heaven. Or a large pepperoni and mushroom pizza. Or… her stomach grumbled in response to her thoughts, which made the entire situation seem even worse. She'd never had to ignore her body's natural reminder for sustenance.

If she was hungry, she ate. It had always been that simple.

Back in the Accord, Meredith aimed the vents in her direction and cranked up the heat. She closed her eyes and breathed through her shivers and chattering teeth, letting the solid stream of warm air soak into her skin and begin to dry her hair and clothes. Just that fast, she regained some of her optimism. She might be hungry, but she certainly wouldn't starve. She had shelter and warmth right here. Even if she was stuck in the car until morning, she would survive.

She would be fine.

With that mantra running through her head, she re-buckled her seat belt, put the car into Drive and cautiously pressed on the gas pedal. The car rocked as the tires fought for traction on the icy layer of snow but didn't actually move forward.

Biting her lip, Meredith applied a miniscule amount of more pressure to the gas pedal and, when that didn't work, a little more yet. The tires spun uselessly for another instant—no more than a second or two—before the car lurched into actual motion. Without conscious thought, she gripped the steering wheel tighter and drove, using the brakes far more often than the gas to retain some semblance of control.

And even her current speed of a sleepy, lazy tortoise felt too fast, too reckless.

She drove slowly, not so much following the road as the dense line of dark trees along either side of the car. As she did, the sun continued its unrelenting descent and the snow kept falling, faster and thicker, decreasing her scant visibility to the point of near blindness. The gusting, rushing gales of wind battered against the car with such ferocious strength that being swept off the road ranked as a real possibility. Terrifying, yes, but also…lonely.

Not in the "oh, I wish I had someone to talk to" sense of lonely, but in the "if this goes bad, I could legitimately die out here, by myself, and no one would know."

Her parents wouldn't have a clue, nor would her brothers or friends or prior coworkers. No one, except for Rachel and her husband, Cole, would even think to try to contact her for days, if not for weeks. She was supposed to be on vacation, after all.

More than that, though. This trip was about a lot more than a simple getaway.

After an inferno of an exchange with her father, Arthur Jensen had made it clear that for the next year, no matter the circumstance she found herself in, he would not intervene. The rest of the family wouldn't, either.

It was what she had wanted, had asked for and then demanded when he'd initially taken her request as a joke. But she hadn't guessed how upset her father would become, the awful truth that slipped out in his anger, which further upset *her* or, when he finally capitulated, the strict set of rules he put in place. She recognized why. He didn't believe she'd agree, but oh, she had. Because really, what else was she to do?

But she certainly hadn't foreseen a freak autumn snowstorm, losing her way in a wholly unfamiliar and apparently remote location or the possibility of death on the horizon. And even if her father could somehow know of her predicament and even if he hadn't declared her as, for all intents and purposes, an orphan for the next year, he couldn't help her now anyway.

No one could.

"Stop it," she said, loud and clear. "I am not going to die out here."

She'd no sooner spoken the words than the faintest shimmer of light appeared ahead and to the right. So faint, she almost wondered if her eyes were playing tricks on her, and what she thought she saw was nothing more than a panic-induced mirage…her personal oasis in the desert. Could be that, she thought, or it could be just as it appeared: a sanctuary. She wouldn't know for sure until she got closer, but hope and relief tempered the rapid beat of her heart.

Neither lasted long. Seemingly out of nowhere, the narrow, uphill road curved sharply to the right and Meredith, in an instinctive attempt to correct her direction, yanked the steering wheel too hard. The car whiplashed to the side before settling into a spin and, now facing the opposite direction, picked up speed and careened downhill.

Gripping the steering wheel even tighter, she worked to keep the car on the road while pumping on the brakes. She couldn't regain control. She closed her eyes, tensed her body and readied herself for whatever came next. Damn it! This should not be happening. She should be with Rachel, sipping wine and trying to let go of the past while deciding on a new and improved future. She was *not* supposed to be lost, scared and…

The impact came hard and swift, jarring her body and ending her inner tirade.

In sync with the crash, a loud noise, almost like a gunshot, rang in Meredith's ears as the airbag deployed and slammed against her chest. An acrid smell, strong and pungent, consumed the interior of the car, along with a powdery dust that coated her face and hair. She might have screamed, if she'd been able to breathe.

Keeping her eyes closed for a minute and then another, she waited for her lungs to kick into gear and her shivers to fade, for her heart to regain its normal rhythm and her stomach to stop sloshing. Finally, when her breathing returned and the starkest edge of her fear ebbed, she opened her eyes. She clenched and unclenched her hands, wiggled her toes and moved her legs.

Okay. Good. All seemed in working order. She hadn't died yet.

Where had those dogs gotten off to? Liam Daly swore under his breath and hollered their names—Max and Maggie—uselessly into the wind tunnel the night had become. They didn't come running, nor could he hear their boisterous barking. Not good.

Not good at all.

It was unusual for them to leave his side in the middle of a storm. Even more unusual for them to do so after he'd been gone for so long.

He'd just returned home after an extended stay in the Aleutian Islands, where he'd photographed a variety of wildlife, including those that lived on the land, flew in the air and swam in the sea. It was a good trip and as always he was thankful for the work, but Lord, he was happy to be back home in Colorado.

He'd be happier if his dogs would show themselves. Max and Maggie were Belgian Tervurens, a shepherding breed closely related to Belgian sheepdogs. They were smart, intuitive, active and more often than not, positioned themselves so close to Liam's legs that he was lucky not to trip over them. They'd done so when they'd first arrived home, after Liam had picked them up from his sister's place in Steamboat Springs proper. Fiona always looked after Max and Maggie when Liam was away, and they loved her almost as much as they loved him.

Fiona had asked him to stay in her guest room for the night, to relax and spend some time with her and her foster daughter, Cassie, due to the oncoming storm. He'd thought about it, because he'd missed them both, but the storm could last for days. Frankly, he'd been away long enough, and he knew the mountains like the back of his own hand.

So, he'd promised his sister and niece—because that was how he thought of Cassie—that he'd visit them soon, and as he'd thought, he didn't have a lick of trouble on the drive home. He'd even made a quick but necessary stop for groceries and still managed to roll into his driveway a solid thirty minutes before the spitting rain had fully turned to sheets of snow-drenched ice.

Knowing his sister would worry, he tried to check in using his mobile, but without a signal, that proved fruitless. And his satellite phone—a necessary piece of technology for assignments in certain remote locations—was pretty much useless with all the trees. Fortunately, and surprisingly, the landline still had service. Wouldn't last much longer, he'd expect, but he was able to reassure Fiona that he'd made it home in one piece.

The dogs had followed as he'd brought in the groceries, turned on the lights and jacked up the heat. They'd gobbled their kibble lightning fast and had then run in circles outside as he lugged in wood for the fireplace.

He'd gotten the fire going before heading out to make sure everything was in order with the generator, because before the night was through, he'd likely lose power. All was good. He had plenty of firewood, propane and food to outlast a storm of mega proportions. He could last a couple of weeks without issue. Good thing, too.

He had that bone-deep intuition that this storm would be one for the history books.

Trying not to worry about the dogs—they knew this part of the mountains as well as Liam did—he hollered their names again while deciding on his next course of action. Likely, the dogs were fine. Wouldn't hurt to give them a bit more time to stretch their legs and find their way home before allowing his concern to rule his judgment.

He'd unpack his equipment, get everything set straight and orderly, so that he could buckle in and work for the next long while. He had hundreds upon hundreds of digital photographs to sort through, analyze, decide which were gold and which were not, in addition to the many rolls of film he had to develop in his darkroom.

It was, perhaps, one of Liam's favorite aspects of his job: the meticulous process of bringing a captured image to life. Oh, he wasn't opposed to technology. Hell, he friggin' loved what technology could do and had done for his profession, both in the practical and artistic sense.

He was, however, a stalwart follower in the church of film photography. He would never want to give up either for the other, but if forced to choose…well, he'd say good-bye to technology and every one of his digital cameras, even his newest Canon, in a nanosecond.

And yeah, he'd be sorry to see them go, but everything about film photography—from the cameras themselves, to how they worked and how to coax the best possible shot out of them, to the art of developing the prints—was what had drawn Liam to this profession to begin with. His want for solitude and exploration drove him toward the obvious niche: nature and wildlife.

Well, also that he tended to understand animals far easier than people. Typically, he liked them better, too. And he would always choose just about any remote location over a city. Cities had too many people, and people liked to talk. Something Liam wasn't all that fond of.

His sister teased him, liked to say that Liam was allergic to other human beings outside of their family network. In a way, he supposed there was some truth to that statement, but his "allergy" was by choice. He was just a guy who did better on his own and had long ago recognized that fact. Other than Fiona and a few friends who didn't annoy him every time they opened their mouths, he had Max and Maggie. Along with his job, that was all he needed.

Calling out their names once again, he waited to see

if they'd show. When they didn't, Liam shoved his worry to the back burner and returned to his cabin.

He'd built it close to five years ago now, on a secluded plot of land that was situated on an equally secluded area of the mountain. He didn't have neighbors. He had trees and streams, wildlife and tons of privacy.

Just as he liked it.

Inside, he shrugged off his coat and boots. If the two shepherds weren't back by the time he was done unpacking his gear, he'd put on his layers of arctic wear and try to track them down. Difficult, maybe impossible, with the current state of the weather, but he would have to try. He wouldn't be able to relax, otherwise.

Making quick work of the job, Liam hauled the equipment to his office at the back of the cabin, taking care to unpack and organize in his standard methodical fashion.

His rolls of exposed film were in airtight, labeled canisters, which he stacked in the refrigerator he kept in this room for just that purpose. A set of customized shelves sat against the back wall that held moisture-proof containers for his various cameras, along with those meant for other necessary items, such as lenses, straps and memory cards. The longest wall of the room held his desk, computers, monitors and an array of additional storage. Everything had a place.

Liam's darkroom was attached to the office, but for the moment, he left that door closed. No reason to go in there until he was ready to begin developing his film, which wouldn't be for another day or two.

With everything more or less put away, he took the stairs two at a time to his bedroom—the only room on the second floor—where he put on the layers of clothing and outerwear appropriate for the howling storm, which was turning into one hell of a blizzard.

Yeah, he had to go after his dogs.

Downstairs, he grabbed a flashlight before opening the front door. Then, having second thoughts, closed it against the torrential slam of wind and snow.

Max and Maggie's favorite roaming grounds were in the dense cluster of trees directly behind the cabin. They'd go round and round, sniffing out squirrels or rabbits, roughhousing with each other and in warmer temperatures, cooling themselves off in the stream that twisted through the trees. He'd go that route first and hope he could outlast the storm long enough to find them and bring them home.

Exiting through the back door, Liam did his best to ignore the worry gnawing at his gut. This just wasn't like them. Unless one of them had gotten hurt somehow, maybe a soft spot in the icy stream held one of them captive or…no. He wouldn't assume worst-case scenario.

They were smart, agile dogs. Excitable and full of energy. Probably, they were happy to be home and, in their canine glee, were ignoring the cold and snow in favor of a frozen romp. Sounded good. Plausible even, to anyone who didn't know Max and Maggie. Problem was, Liam did know them, and that sort of behavior in this type of weather didn't ring true.

He'd find them. He had to. They were as much his family as Fiona and Cassie.

Chapter Two

Within minutes of slamming into a cluster of trees, Meredith realized she no longer heard the comforting hum of the car's engine or felt the warm flow of heat blowing from the vents. She almost turned the key in the ignition to see if the engine would fire again, but had second thoughts. Better to first check out her surroundings and the car's condition.

Shoving the now-deflated airbag off of her body, she unclasped her seat belt, opened the driver's side door and stumbled to her feet. Wind-propelled snow slapped at her face, stinging her skin and making her eyes water. The early evening hung in complete darkness, without so much as a single star shining through to offer even the slimmest ray of light.

In her entire life, she had never felt so alone or unprepared.

She walked the perimeter of where she crashed. Since

she couldn't see more than a foot in front of her, she sniffed the air for signs of a fuel leak. Fortunately, if she could trust her nose, she didn't smell any gas fumes. Assuming the car would start, would she be able to get it back on the road? Maybe. She'd have to be lucky, though. The path out would need to be fairly straightforward, and the car would have to power through the snowy, icy uphill terrain in reverse.

The wall of never-ending wind almost knocked her over, and she had to brace herself to keep standing, had to force her frozen legs to slog through the snow. Again, she was stunned by the saturating, painful depth of the cold. She swore her bones were shivering.

Reaching the back of the car, Meredith tried to gauge how far off the road she'd gone. She couldn't tell, not from where she stood. But with so many trees, she couldn't be too far in. Probably, in the light of day, with or without a storm, she'd be able to see the road from here. As it was, however, attempting to blindly maneuver the car seemed a very bad idea.

Okay, then. Her best course of action was huddling in the Accord for the night. So long as the engine would start, she'd have heat. She had plenty of dry clothes in her suitcase. Oh! She even had a bottle of water and a roll of butter rum–flavored Life Savers. Not the most enjoyable way to spend a night, but it could be worse. A lot worse.

She would be fine.

As she fought her way toward the driver's side door, she suddenly recalled hearing of a woman who—a year or two ago—had died from carbon monoxide poisoning while waiting out a storm in her car. The tailpipes had become clogged with snow, cutting off oxygen. That poor woman had likely also thought she would be safe and sound in the shelter of her car.

Great. Yet another way that Meredith could die tonight.

She retreated again to check the tailpipes. For the moment, the snow wasn't quite high enough to reach them, thank God. Though, at this rate, with the direction the wind was blowing, it wouldn't take too much longer. Then what? She'd have to keep checking.

Satisfied that she'd be safe for the next little while, at least, she finally pushed her frozen, wet and shivering body into the driver's seat. The dry, still somewhat warm interior, even without blowing heat, immediately offered a blessed reprieve. But she'd feel much better with running heat. So, inhaling a large, hopeful breath, she twisted the key in the ignition.

The engine did not rumble to life. Heck, it didn't even squawk. Or whimper. It did nothing. She squeezed her eyes shut and prayed as fervently as she knew how and tried again. Nope. Still nothing. Tears of frustration and fear filled her eyes, but she ignored them.

The good news, she supposed, was that she could cross off carbon monoxide poisoning from tonight's worry list. But the possibility of freezing to death moved up to number one.

Grabbing her iPhone, Meredith pressed the Home button, hoping that between the crash and now, a miracle had somehow occurred and she'd have a signal. And… no to that, as well. She bit her lip hard to stop the fear from taking complete control and leaving her useless.

"Talk through this," she said, finding comfort in the sound of her voice. "What are the options?" There weren't many, so they were easy to count off. "I can stay here, inside the car, out of the storm. Or I can leave and try to find whatever shelter is attached to that light."

Remaining in the car, shielded from the elements, felt

the safer of the two options. She would even bet that was the recommended advice for such a situation. But she didn't fool herself into thinking another motorist would fatefully come along the exact same path, realize she'd crashed, find her and rescue her or that Rachel would send out help—which, okay, she probably already had, but they wouldn't begin to know where to look—or even that she could make it until morning if she hung tight. The hours between now and then seemed endless.

If the storm continued with this force, she could be stuck here for longer than overnight. It could be days. Her car could become buried, the brutal winds could cause a tree to fall, shattering her windshield or trapping her inside.

Or worse.

Beyond all those horrific possibilities, the idea of sitting here, merely waiting for the storm to pass and hoping that nothing dire would occur, did not resonate well. It left too much to chance. It took too much out of her control.

Of course, on the other hand, she really did not relish the thought of going back outside.

Leaving the security of the car, no matter how temporary, required her to fight through the storm, that awful cold, the wind and the mounting snow, with the hope of locating a true shelter. She could fall and hit her head or twist an ankle or become even more lost. Even if she escaped those disasters, she would have to be strong enough to keep moving for however long it took to get somewhere safe. Could she do it? Was she that strong?

With a firmness that surprised her, she came to a decision. Her gut insisted that staying in the car would prove to be a mistake, and really, what else could she trust in but her instincts?

She'd find that light, which had to be connected to a house. And it couldn't be too far away for the glow, as faint as it was, to have made it through the thick, blinding haze of snow.

If she was wrong...no, she wasn't wrong. She *couldn't* be wrong.

In a flurry of adrenaline, Meredith climbed into the back seat and opened her suitcase. She needed dry clothes, layered, something to cover her face, ears and hands. She needed her hiking boots, which would offer a good deal more protection than her perfect-for-traveling, oh-so-cute clogs. And her coat, naturally. On the plus side, she had not packed light.

Sloughing off her wet jeans and sweater—quite the arduous process in the small constraints of the back seat—she put on a pair of leggings she'd planned on sleeping in, followed by one pair of jeans and then another. Over her head, she pulled on a T-shirt, a turtleneck sweater and finally, a long, roomy, extra-thick sweatshirt. Wet socks were replaced with two pairs of warm, dry socks, over which went her hiking boots. Along with her coat, she grabbed another turtleneck, a button-down flannel shirt and two additional pairs of socks.

Before leaving the car, she wrapped the turtleneck around her head and tied the sleeves under her chin. The flannel shirt, she folded and used as a scarf. She hung her purse diagonally over her neck and shoulder, slipped her hands into both pairs of socks and then on top of it all went her coat, which was a struggle of mega proportions to zip.

When all was said and done, she was hot, bulky and uncomfortable, but she thought she'd done a fairly decent job in protecting herself from the elements. Fingers crossed, anyway. As ready as she was going to get, she closed her eyes and breathed. Deeply.

"I will not die out there," she whispered. Opening her eyes, she stepped once again into the icy maelstrom. "I will be strong. I will find the light, which will be attached to a warm and occupied house, and someday in the future this entire night will be nothing more than an awful, distant memory. A story I will tell over drinks."

Right. A story and not the end of her life.

Hunching her shoulders against the wind, Meredith trudged away from the car, keeping her head angled downward and focusing on staying upright.

Her pace was slow, almost sluggish, due to the snow and the wind and the layers of clothing she wore weighing her down. While she had no actual sensation of time, it seemed to take forever to break through the trees and reach the road. So long, in fact, she had a moment of chilling fear that perhaps the car had spun again before the collision and she was walking in the exact wrong direction.

Relief centered in the pool of her stomach that this wasn't the case. Shoving her hands in the pockets of her coat—the socks she'd used as mittens were already wet, leaving her with frozen fingers—she paused to get her bearings. Here, at least, there was zero doubt as to which route to take. Uphill, the way she'd been driving. She'd continue along until she saw that light again. That light would lead her through the storm to safe ground.

Okay. She could do this.

"I am woman, hear me roar," she said into the wind. Silly, maybe, but the words gave her another bolt of strength, of courage. Of belief in herself. Whatever worked, right?

She started the trek, walking smack-dab in the middle of the road, using every muscle in her body to stay upright, all the while pretending that she didn't notice how the cold was seeping through her multiple layers of clothing. Or how her thighs were burning from the exertion. Or how her heart pumped faster, harder, with every labored breath. She kept her gaze glued in the direction she'd seen the light, praying she'd see it again with every step.

So far, just unforgivable darkness.

Had she made a mistake in leaving the car? *No. Don't think like that.* If she had made a mistake, there wasn't a darn thing she could do about that now. What she had to do, all she could do, was keep moving. That was her only job, the only "rule" she needed to follow.

"Don't stop, don't stop, don't stop," she said.

Time melted into a black hole of nothingness. She could've been walking for five hours or five days…she no longer knew. For a good while, her mind remained clear and her focus unfettered by the still-worsening weather or the effect it was having on her body.

But when she realized that it seemed she had gone a farther distance uphill on foot than she had in her car, still with no sign of the glowing light, fear and desperation rode in and took control.

Tears that she'd held back rushed her eyes and clogged her throat. Her legs, frozen and unwieldy, gave in to the demands of the wind and buckled at the knees. She tried to catch herself but couldn't.

Losing her balance, she toppled backward and landed in a heap in the thick, icy snow. She instantly went to stand, but between the weight of her clothes, the ferocious, sharp bite of the wind, the gales of stinging, slashing snow and the unexpected unresponsiveness of her numb limbs, her attempt was met with failure. As were the next three.

She breathed deeply, searched for and found an inner kernel of strength amidst the fear. Of course she could stand. She'd been able to stand for most of her life. It was second nature. It was easy.

She breathed in again, rolled to her knees and planted her hands deep into the snow, until she felt the ground and then, after counting to three, shoved herself up.

She didn't waste time feeling relief or in congratulating herself. This was bad. Worse, even, than she'd let herself believe when she'd ventured from the Honda. Yes, she quite possibly had erred in judgment.

Now, her decision to tread through the storm instead of staying put, where she would have had protection from the wind and snow, felt ludicrous and shortsighted and... well, stupid. Because no, she still did not see that light.

She had been so sure, but could she have imagined it? Perhaps. Especially with her deep desire to locate shelter, yeah, it was possible.

Meredith stopped. Should she turn around and try to find the car? Did that even make sense? The return trip was sure to be easier, since the wind would blow against her back and push her forward, but she wasn't positive she'd be able to locate the car again. Confusion swept in, mixing with her exhaustion and panic, making it nearly impossible to form any decision other than to do just as she was: stand in place. And that...well, that would seal her fate.

Right. Keep moving.

She started to walk again, forcing her body through the unyielding storm, her vision once again aimed in the direction she'd seen the light. If it hadn't been a mirage, she would see it eventually. But she couldn't stop again. No matter what, she couldn't stop.

One step. Two steps. Three, four, five and six.

When she reached ten steps, she started over with one. Anything to keep walking. If she stopped again, that would be that. And she was pretty sure if she fell again, she'd curl up in a ball and close her eyes. Because oh, every ounce of her body yearned for rest.

On her third set of ten steps, acceptance that, yes, she might be facing the last moments of her life seeped in.

How was that possible? How could *this* be it? How could she be *done*? What had she accomplished and what would she be remembered for? What dreams had she fulfilled? Did even one person on the face of the earth really know her?

The answer to that last part came swiftly. How could anyone else really know her when she didn't yet know herself? This trip was supposed to be the official, if belated, start of that journey. A time to make sense of all she'd learned, of what she'd thought was true balanced against the real truth. And then, over the next year, the rest of the pieces would fall into place.

That had been the plan. Not this fight for survival.

Until her early twenties, she hadn't had to fight for much of anything of importance. She and her two brothers were raised in an affluent household. Their parents were strict but attentive. Her childhood was filled with private schools, extensive travel and chauffeur-driven cars. Extracurricular activities were carefully chosen by her parents, and success in school was demanded more than encouraged.

Meredith's grades were always exemplary. She liked to learn, so that part of the equation came naturally. And yes, there were moments she wished her parents would loosen their will in favor of hers, but mostly she towed the line. She went to the college of their choosing, majoring in business as they expected. She fed her love of art with a class here and there, trips to various museums and devoting hours of nonstudy time to sketching and painting.

During her final year of college, she fell head over heels for a man who did not fit in her parents' neat and tidy box of expectations for their only daughter.

Alarico—Rico—Lucio worked as a mechanic, but he had big dreams and, she believed, the will to fulfill them. He drew her into his world quickly, so fast her head spun. He came from a large and boisterous family that had made Meredith feel at home the second she met them. They accepted her without question, as one of their own, simply because she was Rico's girlfriend.

And with love, everything changed. For the first time in Meredith's life, she had something to fight for. A future she wanted with a man she adored. She hoped that given enough time, her parents would come around and embrace her relationship with Rico, just as his family had.

There was a short period where she believed they tried and that they wanted her to be happy. Rico saw it differently, though, and he worried that eventually, their relationship would cause irreparable harm between her and her parents. He refused to separate Meredith from her family, and he refused to be viewed as a second-class citizen. Two strikes, not three.

But they were brutal strikes.

He ended their relationship, swearing that he would love her forever, and that someday, he would return to her as a man her family would respect and honor. His words were heartfelt, his voice sincere…his decision final.

The best year of her life ended in her greatest heart-break. She blamed her parents and their unrealistic ide-als of perfection for pushing Rico away. She blamed her brothers for their choice in "acceptable" mates, and she blamed the universe.

She missed Rico. Her heart ached for him, but she re-spected his decision and did not try to contact him. There was some pride there, as well. She'd hoped he'd miss her as much as she missed him, give up on his insistence to wait and come to her. He did not.

After graduation, she found some backbone and in-stead of going to work for her father as had been the orig-inal plan, landed the stager position with little trouble. Surprising, really, since she had a degree in business, but oh, had she been happy. The job paid more than the going rate, which pleased her, and she found a small but nice apartment to live in.

For the next handful of years, she'd worked hard to create a life that she believed was of her own making. She'd been happy, except for missing Rico. She never stopped hoping that one day he would reach whatever level of success he needed and come back to her as he'd promised.

She had *waited* for him, day in and day out, for… years. Her heart held hostage, her hopes in limbo. And all for nothing. Absolutely nothing. None of it was real.

As it turned out, her job wasn't real, either. Well, the work was, she supposed, but she hadn't gotten the job on her own accord. The great and mighty Arthur Jensen had paved the way and was even "helping" with Mere-dith's salary. Tidbits of information that a tipsy coworker with loose lips had accidentally slipped at a company get-together less than three weeks ago.

She hadn't aced the job interview to win the job. She

hadn't *earned* her bonuses over the years. All she was, all she'd ever been, was the privileged daughter of a successful man who had the leverage and the will to pull the right strings at the right time.

The second she confirmed the information was true, she quit her job. Then, humiliated and angry, resentful, too, she confronted her father. Initially, he'd tried to pacify her, but as their argument grew more heated, he called her "soft and sheltered" and stated that if he hadn't stepped in, she wouldn't have survived a year.

In a burst of emotion, she told her father that she was tired of living a life that he deemed appropriate and that due to him, she'd lost Rico. The best man she'd ever known. That it was his fault. Because her father had been blind to her happiness, because all he saw was a man with a blue-collar job who came from a blue-collar family, and wouldn't that be embarrassing, to have to introduce Rico—a mechanic—as his daughter's boyfriend? Or worse, as his son-in-law?

Her father wasn't a warm and cuddly man, but he wasn't a cruel man, either. No, Arthur Jensen was a decisive man. He formed decisions quickly, based on all available information combined with a high-functioning intuition, and he rarely backed down. Meredith's words, along with her emotional state, must have hit a nerve. After years of staying silent, her father told her the truth about the man she claimed to love.

Rather than accepting an entry-level position at one of Arthur's companies—which Meredith hadn't known was even offered at the time—Rico turned the tables. He promised he would walk out of Meredith's life, never to return, for the sum of $50,000. Otherwise, he would marry her and within a year, she'd have one child and be pregnant with another.

Disgusted with Rico but seeing the man spoke the truth, her father paid the money, and Rico did exactly as he'd promised. Broke off their relationship and disappeared.

Her father had proof in his safe—the cashed check and a signed statement from Rico—but Meredith did not require that confirmation. Her father wouldn't lie about something so terrible. Her heart had cracked in agony again as she realized all the emotion, time and energy she'd wasted on Alarico and her ridiculous dreams for the future.

The only love she'd ever known had been false. The job she'd worked hard at for years, had believed she'd earned on her own merits, ranked as another false belief. On their own, these two were enough to swing the pendulum, but when she considered how often she'd followed her parents' wishes over her own, she was…done. Done being the privileged daughter of a successful man. Done living her life by someone else's set of expectations and rules.

More arguing ensued before she got what she wanted: zero interference. She also got what she hadn't asked for in the way of zero contact with her family. For a period of one year. She hadn't expected that stipulation, and it hurt, but she held her chin high and agreed.

It was time—more than time—to build a life she could trust in.

The following seven days were a mix of self-recrimination, doubts and insecurities as she attempted to pull herself out of the muck and consider her options for the future. That was when she contacted Rachel, a close friend who had grown up in the same affluent world as Meredith. Of all her friends, Rachel was the only one who was sure to understand the importance of Meredith's decision. And why she absolutely had to succeed.

It was decided that Meredith would use some of her savings to spend a few weeks vising Rachel in Steamboat Springs, Colorado. In addition to rest and relaxation and letting her brewing emotions settle, the reprieve would offer the opportunity to come up with an achievable plan. Where to live? Where to work? What dreams to chase?

To think she'd put so much energy into proving that she could make it on her own. An idealistic notion that, while important in a lot of ways, felt ridiculous and meaningless now that her life hung in the balance. *This* was the only fight that mattered. Survival.

And it was all on her.

Her thoughts ended when her knees buckled against the strong wind for a second time. She managed to stay standing, but it was by the skin of her teeth. Still no sign of that light, and she knew—in the way a person *knows*—that she did not have much left in her.

Lord. She was really going to die out here. Alone.

Why bother trying for another step, let alone ten, when her body, heart and brain all knew the truth? She wouldn't find that light. She wouldn't reach safety. She didn't know how long it would take, but yes, death was pounding on her door. Soon, not much longer, she guessed, he'd kick down the door and that would be that. And she would take her last breath. Have her last thought. Perhaps, if she had the strength, she'd cry her last tear.

So why bother? Why not just drop to the ground and… no. No!

She wasn't about to give up until she was left with no other choice. And no matter how close that moment might be, she wasn't there yet. She'd fight for as long as she could. Simple as that.

"Help me," she whispered the prayer. "Send an angel to guide me. Please?"

A sound other than the howling wind made it to her ears. What was that? She stopped, listened harder and heard the sharp, abrupt noise again and then again. It sounded like barking.

A dog? Yes. Had to be a dog.

More barking, and it seemed to be growing closer. Where there was a dog, there was probably a human. An actual person! Meredith turned in a circle, trying to gauge which direction the sounds were coming from. Close, she thought, but…where?

Oh, God, show me where.

"Help!" she called out, hoping her voice would cut through the storm as cleanly as the dog's continuous series of barks. "Help me, please! I'm—"

Through the darkness a dog emerged, followed by another, both barking and moving far swifter than she would've thought possible. And then, they were at her side. *Two* dogs, not one. They were covered in snow, whining now instead of barking, and one started nipping at her ankles while the other mouthed her sock-covered hand and tugged.

"Hello?" she yelled. "Your dogs are with me! Hello?"

No response other than the dogs, who were still whining and nipping and tugging. Were they out here alone? She hollered into the wind again and waited, watched to see if anyone would answer or a human figure would emerge from the same direction the dogs had.

And…no.

Okay. Okay. Her salvation wasn't right around the corner. The dogs had probably gotten loose and were trying to find their own way back home. She could barely keep herself standing. What was she to do with two dogs who were likely just as lost as she was?

Still. They were company. She was no longer alone.

"Hey, guys," she said, her voice weak. "I'm happy to see you, but I'm afraid I'm not going to be of much help. I have no idea where I am or where you two came from."

The dog that was nipping at her heels stopped for a second to growl. Softly, not menacingly, and then returned to gently prodding at her heels. The dog who had her hand tugged harder and whined plaintively. As if to say, "Come on! Pay attention to what we're doing! Don't just stand there. Get moving! Lead us to safety, why don't you?"

"I don't know where safety is," she said. Tears flooded her eyes. "I wish I did."

Dropping her hand, the dog barked and ran ahead a few feet. Faced her and barked again. The other dog barked, too, and then shoved its head against the back of her legs, toward dog number one.

She stumbled from the pressure, almost fell, but the pooch pushed to her side and she grabbed onto its fur for stability and managed to keep herself standing.

Her numb brain clicked into gear. Were they trying to get her to move? Were they trying to lead *her* to safety? That was how it seemed, and because she needed something to believe in, to propel her into action, she chose to accept that these dogs were her saviors and all she had to do was follow them. Trust in them to get her out of this mess.

So she did.

Once the dogs saw she was walking, one stayed at her side while the other would run up a few feet, stop and bark until she made her way to that position. Over and over, this pattern was repeated. She almost fell a few times, but by the grace of God and the dog beneath her hand, she didn't. The storm wailed on, the cold grew even more bitter, and she knew that if not for these dogs— angels, they were angels—she wouldn't have made it this long.

She would have fallen. And this time, she would not have gotten back up.

Suddenly, Dog A—the one setting their direction— started barking even more exuberantly, and that was when Meredith saw the light.

She hadn't imagined it!

With tremendous effort, she pushed herself forward, watched the dog run ahead a few more feet, and she pushed herself again. A house! An actual house. She could see the outline now.

She was so close that she was almost on top of it.

The storm had grown increasingly worse since she'd first seen the porch light, before her accident. She should have realized that by the time she returned to approximately the same position on foot, the snow would've fully camouflaged the glow. She wouldn't have seen it again. Not on her own, not without these dogs. But here it was. Just a few more feet.

That was all she had to walk, all she had to find enough power for. A few more feet.

They were, without doubt, the most difficult, exhausting few feet that Meredith had ever walked. But she made it to the porch, up the few steps and to the door.

The dogs were on either side of her now, pressing their bodies against her legs, sharing their strength. Keeping her standing. She knocked on the door, but her fist barely made a sound. She tried again and then, knowing she was this close to collapse, turned the doorknob and pushed open the door.

She called out a feeble "Hello?" but received no response. The room—the blessedly warm room—was empty. The dogs left her side to run in, barked at her to follow and so...well, she did. Unless the owner of this house was heartless, he or she would most certainly understand. And if they didn't? Well, that was the last worry on Meredith's mind.

Closing the door behind her, she tried for another "Hello" before half stumbling her way across the room. A low-burning, welcoming fire glowed brightly from the fireplace, and a long, inviting couch was right there along the wall. She went to the sofa, knowing she should take off her coat and outer layers of clothing, but...she couldn't.

As in, she was unable to.

All she could do was sit down, and then stretch out, on the thick, comfortable cushions and stare at the fire. Oddly, she did not feel awkward at being in a stranger's home without permission. She wasn't worried if the owner would understand or be angry when he or she walked in. All she felt, through and through, was a deep, abiding sense of relief.

Just relief. But it was profound.

Meredith fought to stay awake so that when the mystery owner appeared, she could try to explain her presence. Probably, she should sit up. Thought again that she should take off her coat, the shirts wrapped around her head, the socks on her hands. But doing so seemed impossible. Doing so would require considerably more energy than she currently had available.

So she closed her eyes, breathed in the deliciously warm air, and thanked the good Lord for getting her this far. She was alive. Freezing, exhausted, shivering and numb...but *alive*.

A miracle had occurred. She was not going to die tonight.

Vaguely, she felt the pressure of the dogs—her angels—as they jumped onto the sofa and snuggled their bodies around her, again offering what protection, what help they could. And that was enough to put an end to her feeble resistance. She stopped trying to find energy where there was none, stopped thinking altogether and allowed her body to do what it demanded.

She slept.

Chapter Three

For a solid hour and a half, Liam searched for Max and Maggie. They weren't behind the house, nor were they at the stream. He branched out in an ever-widening circle around the cabin while keeping track of his own position. At the forty-five-minute mark, he promised himself he'd only give it another fifteen before returning home, even though he flat-out hated the idea of stopping.

The dogs had gotten stuck somewhere, or one of them was injured. There just wasn't another logical explanation for their absence. And he had no doubt that if something had happened to one, the other would stand sentry. His dogs were loyal beyond belief, to each other, to him, to Fiona and Cassie. Hell, they'd probably be loyal to a stranger, so long as that stranger wasn't causing them or their family harm. They were those sorts of dogs.

So when he hit an hour without any sign of them, he gave himself another thirty minutes. Due to the storm and all it brought with it, it was slowgoing despite his knowledge of the terrain and his attempts to move quickly. Didn't matter where he looked, though. They had seemingly vanished.

It was possible they'd returned to the cabin while he was trekking over the mountainside and even now were waiting for *his* return. He hoped so.

But yeah, another half an hour before turning back.

At one point, through the wind, he thought he heard barking, but it was so faint and so distant, he couldn't determine the direction. He called out their names repeatedly and listened closely.

Nothing.

Just the noisy storm playing tricks with his ears, fueled by his desperate hope to locate his dogs. Sighing, Liam pushed forward for the allotted thirty more minutes before turning on his heel and heading back toward the cabin with that awful, sick sloshing in his gut.

If they weren't there, he'd do the smart thing and warm up, get some food in him, rest for an hour or so, before beginning the search anew. And he'd rinse and repeat those actions for as long as it took or until his body gave out on him and he required more than an hour rest in between. Experience had taught him that he could go a real long time with minimal rest.

As he approached the house, he kept his eyes peeled for signs of Max and Maggie, willing them to appear. They did not. Nor were they waiting for him near the back door.

Damn it!

It was difficult to not turn around and retrace every one of his steps, but he knew better. This storm was fierce. As much as he wanted to get his dogs, he needed intermittent breaks in order to keep going throughout the night. Otherwise, he faced the possibility of wearing himself out too soon, which wouldn't do Max or Maggie a lick of good.

Sighing, feeling the weight of the world upon his shoulders, Liam entered through the back door, stopping in the heated mudroom. Piece by piece, he removed his outerwear, starting with his insulated gloves, coat and pants and ending with his heavy-duty hiking boots. Next came the wool hat and the midlayer, which was basically a fleece track suit. He hung each item separately, so all would be dry and ready to wear when he ventured back out.

Wearing only his socks, thermal-compressed long johns and a long-sleeved shirt, he walked into the kitchen, his plan to start a pot of coffee. While that brewed, he'd go upstairs, put on a fresh base layer and then prepare a meal. He wasn't tired yet, so he didn't need a nap. No more than an hour's reprieve should do the trick, less if he could get away with it.

He measured the coffee, filled the pot's reservoir with water, clicked the power button, and as he completed each step, he considered where to start his next foray. If the dogs were stuck or hurt anywhere nearby, he felt sure he would've found them. So, they were either farther out than seemed reasonable or, somehow, they'd been picked up by a passing motorist who just happened to be driving through this remote area in the middle of a friggin' storm.

Doubtful, though not impossible.

Running his hands over his eyes, Liam released a worried sigh. When he woke that morning, all had been right with the world—his world, anyhow—and now, because of two lost dogs, every last thing felt slightly skewed, just enough off balance to be completely wrong. If he'd accepted Fiona's offer of staying at her place through the storm, he'd still have his dogs.

All would have remained right in his world.

He stomped out that thought good and fast. One of the many lessons he'd learned over the years was not to dwell on what couldn't be changed. What-ifs did not yield results. All what-ifs did was fill a person with regret, making them wish for the impossible. And that right there was a huge waste of brainpower, energy, and productivity.

Smarter, better to learn from where you've already walked, but focus on the ground ahead of you that has not yet been covered.

Fifteen minutes gone. Liam strode from the kitchen into the living room, his vision planted directly on the stairs. Change clothes. Eat. Drink coffee. Get back out there, and…whoa.

Halting with one foot half raised in the air in front of the first step, he pivoted toward the sofa. There were his dogs, safe and sleeping so soundly that neither raised their sharp, pointed noses in his direction.

For a fraction of a second, all Liam could do was stare in shock. How the hell had they gotten into the house? Had they somehow followed him in earlier and he hadn't noticed? In another millisecond, as his shock faded into relief, he realized they were not alone.

A slight, huddled figure—a woman, he thought—was curled tight against the back of the sofa. Maggie rested at the tips of a pair of petite hiking books and Max stretched out on his stomach along the length of the stranger's body.

Liam went to the couch, knelt down and patted Max's head before reaching over to gently shake the woman's dark-gray-coat-covered shoulder. She didn't budge or make a sound. He tried again with the same result.

Sizing up the situation and not liking what he saw— wet coat and jeans, pale skin, slight shivers rippling through the woman's body—Liam muffled a curse. Max, hearing Liam, opened his eyes and scooted to join his sister at the end of the sofa. He whined in an imploring fashion, pushed his nose into the woman's denim-clad leg and whined again.

"I know, boy," Liam said. "I know."

There were a few scenarios that came to mind, but the precise details of how this woman got to his couch escaped him. He also did not know how long she'd been roaming in the bitter cold before finding her way here. Neither of those mattered at that moment. What did was determining the state of her health, along with that of his dogs.

Questions could be answered later.

"Max. Maggie," he said sharply. "Down!" Max obeyed instantly, but Maggie kept sleeping, so Liam gently tugged her ear. She shifted, opened her eyes and yawned. He repeated his command, and she slid to the floor, where she stood next to Max and added her canine voice to his in a whine equally as imploring. "I got her," Liam said. "Promise."

The tense lines of the dogs' bodies relaxed as they plopped their butts on the floor, both sets of eyes now bright and alert, focused on the prone woman. Apparently relieved to pass on the caretaking duty to Liam but unwilling to drop their protective vigil until whatever danger they sensed had passed.

"I got her," Liam repeated. The dogs retreated to the thick rug in front of the fireplace, where they landed on their bellies. Both sets of eyes continued to watch, assess.

He gently rolled the woman to her back and tried to wake her again. Her eyes remained firmly shut, her breathing a little too fast for his comfort. He also wasn't fond of the whiter-than-milk shade of her skin.

Hypothermia? Quite possibly, and if so, hopefully not too far advanced. And yeah, he knew what he had to do, he just didn't want to without her permission. Which she couldn't give unless she woke the hell up.

"Hey, there," he said, squeezing her hand as he spoke. "I'm Liam and my dogs are Max and Maggie. We're… ah…happy you're here, safe. And I'm guessing this is the most comfortable you've been in a good long while, but I would greatly appreciate it if you'd open those eyes of yours. Maybe talk to me for a few minutes, answer some of my questions."

She did not even flinch.

He set his discomfort aside and, moving quickly, unzipped her coat. "Okay, I get it. You don't want to be disturbed. No problem for the moment, but if you can hear me," he said, keeping his voice at an even, calm keel, "I need to get all of these wet clothes off of you. I'm sorry about this, but don't be scared. I'm trying to help, not hurt."

Doubtful she heard him, but it seemed better somehow, saying the words.

He took off the wet socks covering her hands, removed her coat, unlaced and yanked her boots from her feet and—feeling like a peeping tom, even knowing he had to do it—unclasped and unzipped her cold, wet jeans.

Ah. Smart woman, she had on another pair underneath. Also cold, also wet. When both pairs were tugged from her body, leaving her in a pair of thin black leggings—they would also have to come off, but not yet—he pushed out a strangled breath.

Turning his attention to the rest of her body, ignoring the rapid beat of his heart—she hadn't moved a muscle, even as her jeans were removed—he untied the shirts she'd wrapped around her head and face, exposing a tumble of long, curly, matted blond hair. And he had that weird déjà vu sensation that he'd been here, done this before.

She, this, reminded him of... "Goldilocks," he muttered. "Asleep on my couch, rather than my bed, but close enough. Guess that means I'm one of the three bears."

Of course, his sister would say he was grumpy enough to be all three bears in one.

Trying not to jar Goldi too much, he lifted her upper body with one arm and unhooked her purse from her shoulder, taking it over her head. Her black sweatshirt and the turtleneck she wore under it were both wet. It took some doing, but he got those off, too. Now, Miss Goldilocks was down to a T-shirt, leggings and socks. And she still hadn't moved.

A thick, soft blanket was folded over the back of the sofa. Covering her with it, he said, "I need to get a few things, darlin', but I'll only be a couple of minutes. Why don't you try to open your eyes while I'm gone? Would make me and the dogs very, very happy."

Upstairs first, for dry clothes—she'd drown in them, as they were his, but he figured she wouldn't mind—and next, the linen closet for several more blankets. As expected, when he returned, Max and Maggie had jumped on the sofa, taking their prior positions at her feet and alongside her. And the sight of this, for some unknown reason, made his heart pound a mite harder. Warmed it a little, too.

"Down," he said, motioning his arm toward the floor. They didn't obey instantly, just whined and gave him *that* look. Not a surprise, really. Now that they'd shaken off their tundra expedition and had warmed themselves by the fire, their stubborn streak had intensified. "Down," Liam repeated, in a firm, don't-argue-with-me tone. They complied.

But they didn't return to the fire. They stood as close to the sofa as possible without actually being on it, watching Goldi with acute alertness. In some way Liam did not yet understand, his dogs had bonded with this woman. She was theirs now. One of the pack.

Unexpected. Curious, too.

Liam sighed and finished what he had started. Reminding himself that he was taking *care* of her and not taking advantage, he used the blanket that was already covering her as a privacy tent of sorts.

He reached underneath and slipped off her leggings, replacing them with a pair of his drawstring pajama bottoms, which he tied at her waist. Rinse and repeat with her T-shirt and one of his sweatshirts, although this switcheroo proved a bit more complex. He did the same with her feet, shucking off her wet socks—two pairs— and covering them with a single pair of his thick, wool socks. Finally, he gathered the blankets he'd brought downstairs, and one by one, layered them on top of her, using one to tuck around her head.

Now that she was dry, clothed and covered, he tried once again to rouse her to awareness. While she did not fully open her eyes, her lashes fluttered slightly and a soft moan fell from her lips.

That seemed positive, and far better than complete unresponsiveness. But she was still shivering. Her breathing remained rapid, though perhaps less so than earlier, and when he checked her pulse, he found it steady if a bit fast. She was also still too pale for his peace of mind.

She needed hydration. Something warm, sweet, and caffeine free. Liam wasn't much for sweet or caffeine free, but Fiona kept a few boxes of herbal teas here for when she visited. He'd brew a cup of that, add a little sugar, and spoon it into Goldi's mouth. He couldn't give her much, as she was still unconscious, but even a little would help. He'd take it slow. Which meant that he had one long night ahead of him, because—much like his dogs—he wouldn't leave his surprise houseguest's side until he knew she was okay or, he supposed, was on the definite road to being okay.

Max woofed a soft, impatient bark. A whine from Maggie followed. Looking at his anxiously waiting dogs, Liam nodded toward the sofa. They seemed fine physically, but after the tea, he'd give them a thorough once-over to reassure himself.

"Go ahead," he said. "I won't stop you now. Your body warmth will do her good."

That was all they needed to hear. Thirty seconds later, Maggie was curled around Goldi's feet and Max was stretched out beside her. In almost perfect unison, they heaved breaths of relief while giving Liam a look that seemed to say, "Okay! Good! What's next?"

Great question. "We need her to wake up. Work on that, while I make the tea."

She'd been cold. So very cold, yet her exhaustion had overpowered the need to find warmth. Sleeping was easier, made her forget about the cold.

A voice, soothing and rich, layered and evocative, had chiseled into her brain, asking her to wake up. And oh, she tried to do as the voice asked, tried to find the will to rouse herself and talk, because it seemed of utmost importance to whomever spoke that she do so.

But try as she might, she couldn't. It was as impossible as taking flight, using her arms as wings. So, she fell deeper into the realm of the unconscious, where her mind concocted a fairy tale to explain all she felt, all she heard.

In her dream, there wasn't a blizzard raging outside. It was the middle of summer, one of those perfect balmy days that smelled of coconuts and lime, with fluffy cotton clouds floating in a robin's-egg-blue sky. She was on a boat, drifting aimlessly, listening to the lapping waves and enjoying the luxurious rays of the sun as they coated her naked body in the most delectable warmth. Hands, also warm and soothing, brushed gently against her skin—her legs, her arms, her face—and every now and then, stroked her hair.

She hadn't felt safe in so long. Why? She couldn't remember the details, but tendrils of nausea swirled in her belly. *Now*, though, she felt safe and protected and so gloriously, wonderfully warm.

Again, the stranger's tenor sifted into the smoky film of her dreams, where it sparked and sizzled in her soul. Her brain decided that this deep and evocative voice must belong to the man who loved her and that he was, in some form or fashion, taking care of her.

Had she been ill? Her stomach rocked with another bout of nausea. Seasick, she determined. While the softly bobbing boat spoke of calm waters now, it must have been rough going earlier. And this man with his delicious voice had seen her through the worst of it. So, yes, he loved her.

Did she love him? She couldn't see his face, recall his name or even how they had met, but for her to feel so absolutely safe and cared for, love had to exist on both sides.

She continued to sleep, continued to dream. Lost to

reality. There was nothing to worry about, not a reason on earth to force herself awake.

Slipping deeper into this magnificent dream world, her subconscious manufactured the type of love only found in the most romantic of movies, with her and the man behind the gentle touches and seductive voice as the leads. She still couldn't remember his face, which was odd, yes, but somehow, this lack of knowledge didn't cause her a moment's concern. He was hers. She was his. That was enough.

But suddenly, she saw his eyes. And oh, were they gorgeous. Sensual and vivid and striking. Distinctive. Irises rimmed in dark olive green that gradually lightened to the color of moss near his pupils, glinted with shots of burnished gold and warm brown. Eyes she *knew*.

They belonged to the man she loved.

And with this man at her side, her brain continued to weave a story for her alone to experience. There was laughter and passion. Long talks and handheld walks. A proposal and then a wedding. Children, a boy and a girl named Max and Maggie.

Years upon years passed while she slept, years filled with the purest form of happiness she'd ever known. Satiating, complete, fulfilling and robust. Ever changing, ever growing, ever stronger…day in and day out.

This fantasy was so intense, so real, so exhilarating and breathtaking, so *beautiful* a life her mind had created, that even as she started to come around, to realize she was merely dreaming, she staunchly resisted the pull of awareness. She wanted, yearned for more of this.

Precisely, *this* life. And she wasn't ready to leave it behind.

The sad truth was that even with Rico, before learning that all of his words had been bald-faced lies, she hadn't known such depths of emotion existed. So, she stubbornly held on to her dream world and tried—oh, how she tried—to quiet her thoughts, relax her body, to return to the fantasy. But with conscious thought of Rico, her fog-filled brain cleared and the rest of the facts from the past several weeks engulfed her in a rush.

Her job. The argument with her father. Deciding to visit Rachel and flying to Colorado. Her decision to rent a car and then losing her way in the mountains. The storm. The accident. Her loneliness and consuming fear, the acceptance that she would die...and then, those dogs.

Those astounding dogs who'd found her and led her to shelter. Had led her...here.

No. She did not want to think about any of that, had no desire to do anything other than fall back into a coma-like sleep and return to that oh-so-beautiful life. Pretend or not, it didn't matter. She yearned to be there again, even if every speck of it was only her imagination.

But the voice that had started it all was becoming more insistent that she wake. *Now.* That she'd been sleeping for too long and enough was enough. That she open her mouth and drink, because she needed more than a spoonful or two of tea every hour. He was tired. He was worried.

"Open your eyes, Goldi," he said, his voice loud and commanding. "Now!"

She did *not* obey his command. Eventually, she would have to, but at the moment, she didn't need to look into this man's eyes and see they weren't green with golden flecks. They were probably brown. And while she did not have a thing in the world against brown eyes, she wasn't ready to give up her fantasy. This man's voice—his deliciously rich voice—was, in her mind, a matching set to the green eyes she'd imagined.

To see otherwise would only make it more difficult to jump into her dream life when she was able to sleep again, and she believed she'd be able to soon. If only he would stop *talking*.

"Goldilocks, you're killing me here," the man said in a lower volume. "Wake. Up."

She still would not have responded except for the identifiable set of canine whines that followed his plea. *Her dogs.*

Sighing, unwilling to ignore her angels, she capitulated enough to say, "I'm awake." A tail thumped near her leg as she spoke. A warm nose pressed against her cheek, giving her a lavish lick. "Kind of."

Ouch. His voice might be a melody fit for a concert, but hers sounded rough and raspy. Thick. Nothing like normal. As if she hadn't spoken aloud in days.

"Thank God," he half whispered. Then, "Great! I knew you could do it. How about opening your eyes and trying to sit up? Move slowly, though. You've been out for a while."

Those words acted as a catalyst, and suddenly, she realized how heavy and cumbersome her body—as in, every inch of it—felt. Tipping her head in the opposite direction of the man's voice, because no, she still wasn't ready to see him, she did as he asked and waited for her blurry vision to sharpen. She stared at the back of a couch, at the thick stripes of deep burgundy, gold and forest green on the cushion. She remembered how she'd stumbled across the room on unwieldy legs, frozen and exhausted, with this piece of furniture as her singular goal.

She had almost died. *Almost.*

"You said I have been out for a while," she said. "How long is that, exactly?"

"I don't know the precise moment you found your way here and collapsed." Muted frustration, perhaps some concern, echoed in his speech. "When I came home, you were already down for the count, but we're going on close to twenty-four hours since then."

How was that possible? In reality, an entire night and another day had elapsed, yet in her dreams, that same amount of time had equaled years. She thought about the picture she must have presented to this man, a stranger, as he'd walked into his living room with her passed out on his couch. She was lucky. So very lucky. He could've been a monster.

"I'm sorry about letting myself in and…well, I mean, I knocked first and I tried to stay awake, but…I should've tried harder." Though, even as she said the words, she knew there wasn't any *trying harder*. She'd barely made it this far. "So, um, I'm sorry."

With each word, her voice grew in strength, became more sure, but still held that rough and raspy edge. *Thirsty.* Lord, she was thirsty. And she had to pee, too. Badly, though not as desperately as one would think after sleeping for a full twenty-four hours.

He snorted. "You're forgiven for saving your life. I'd have done the same."

"You…took care of me, too." She knew he'd stripped off her clothes, redressed her in something else, had dribbled tea into her mouth. It was a lot to do for a stranger. "Thank you."

"Didn't have much choice," he said in a brusque but not unkind manner. "There's no way to get help out here until the storm is over and the roads are cleared. From the looks of it, we'll be stuck together for another handful of days. Maybe a week. But you're welcome."

"A week?"

"Unlikely, but possible. So, if you hadn't found your way here, well…"

Right. She would have died. She'd already figured that one out. Pretending she felt better than she did, she said, "If we're going to be stuck together, I'd like to know your name."

"Oh, sorry. It's Liam. And it will be fine. Number one priority is your health."

So far, he hadn't pushed her to do *anything* now that she was awake and talking. He had to be exhausted, but he was giving her the opportunity to orient herself. To figure out how she felt and how to find some comfort in this strange situation. Unless, of course, he often had strangers stumbling to his house in the middle of a storm and passing out on his sofa.

For some reason, the thought made her laugh.

"What's so funny, Goldilocks?"

"Meredith," she corrected, "And…" Oh. Okay. That small, barely there laugh had magnified the pressure on her bladder tenfold.

Saying a mental goodbye to that beautiful, love-filled—and not to mention, pretend—life she'd concocted, Meredith planted her hands on the couch and slowly pushed into a sitting position. The dog who had been squashed against her side jumped off the couch but not before gracing her with another doting lick to her cheek. "This is awkward," she said, "but I need to use the bathroom."

"No need to feel awkward, and of course you do," he said, his voice reasonable. "I'll show you where it is, but be careful when you stand. Take it slow."

"Right." Her head swam for a minute, maybe two, before she regained her equilibrium. Time to face the music, time to look into this man's real eyes.

She turned to face him. And her breath caught in her

throat, her heart ramped up in speed and a tremble of surprise rolled through her weakened limbs as she stared into Liam's eyes.

Green and gold, sensual and vivid, striking and distinctive. The same eyes she'd dreamed about. But they were real, not imaginary, and they belonged to Liam-with-the-rich-and-layered-voice.

And oh, the rest of what she saw lived up to those eyes. Wavy black hair, somewhat tousled at the moment, framed a strongly featured face that all but begged to be touched. The chiseled, powerful line of his cheekbones was a work of freaking art, as was the firm, somewhat generous stretch of his lips. His nose was mostly straight, neither too large nor too small, and a square, powerful jaw that suggested inherent stubbornness completed the picture. Her fingers itched to sketch this man, to bring his likeness to life on the page.

Without doubt, though, it was Liam's eyes that resonated with her soul. They brought to the surface how, in her dreams, this man had been *hers*, and she had been his.

"I dreamed you," she blurted, lost as their "life" came back to her in waves. "I dreamed us. And you're going to think I'm crazy, but I'm supposed to be here, with you. Because this is how we meet, and there must be a meeting before anything else can happen. And a lot is going to happen for us." Great. She had to sound like a nutcase. "Or…um…I meant to say that in my dream, a lot happened. But you know, not until after we met. Which makes sense!"

Confusion darted into those stunning eyes of his, followed quickly by concern. "Is that so?" he asked lightly. "Well, before you explain any more of that, how about we get you to the bathroom? Once you're set there, your body needs sustenance. I'll whip up something that resembles a meal. After that, you'll probably feel a lot better. More like yourself."

Ha. He thought she was delirious. And okay, she probably shouldn't rule out that possibility. But if there was any chance at all that she'd dreamed about a life—an incredible, beautiful life—with this man for a reason, then she had to consider what that reason could be. The pull to do so was strong. Stronger than she thought she could, or even should, resist.

Though, he was right on one front: she'd wait and see how she felt about everything later, once she'd shaken off more of the dream world in favor of the real world.

This world. The one she was apparently stuck in for... oh, maybe a week. With a man whose eyes seared her soul.

It would prove interesting, to say the least. It might even be life changing.

Chapter Four

Liam needed to sleep. Soon. The grouch in him was crawling to the surface, and the last thing he wanted to do was bite this poor woman's head off. She'd already been through enough. Before he could give into his body's demand for rest, though, he had to be certain Goldi—*Meredith*—wasn't about to pass out again. She required food far more than he did sleep.

Even if his body declared otherwise.

He waited outside the bathroom door, listening for signs of distress or cries for assistance. So far, all he heard was the full blast of the water faucet as she, presumably, tended to some hygiene matters. After she ate, he'd get her another set of clothes and show her where the bath towels were, as he imagined she'd like a shower. Hell, he'd like one of those, too.

She had dreams about him, she'd said, and that she was supposed to be here, that a meeting had to happen before anything else could, and that a lot was going to happen. Made him worry she'd bonked her head, though he hadn't noticed any bruising or, for that matter, lumps or bumps.

What if she was delusional? Dealing with an extra person with their sanity intact, stuck in the same space—*his* space—would prove challenging enough for a guy like him, but if she kept rambling on about dreams? Well, he'd rather not deal with any of that nonsense, thank you very much.

Not that he had any other option, he supposed. She was here for the next good while, and there wasn't a damn thing he could do about it.

Combing his fingers through his hair, Liam tried to keep his impatience under wraps. Wasn't her fault she ended up in his vicinity during a freakishly early storm. Wasn't her fault that she'd dreamed whatever she had. More than likely, once she ate and rested again, she'd be closer to her normal self. Which, hopefully, would be defined as the non-annoying type.

That, he could handle. He'd been dealing with that most of his life.

Finally, the water turned off, and a few seconds later, the door creaked open. Lord, she was pale. And the purple smudges under her eyes spoke of her exhaustion. Maybe she'd eat, take that shower, and sleep for another twelve hours. A likely scenario. Hell, she'd probably sleep most of the next week, which meant they'd barely have to exchange words.

He felt a whole lot better at that thought. It would be almost as if she wasn't even here.

Until she slept again, though, this would be awkward as hell. Sighing, Liam gestured toward the sofa. "You're going to be weak for a while. Rest. I'll bring you some food and…ah…more tea. Unless you'd rather have something cold? I have grape juice or—"

"Yes, please." She leaned into the wall for support and a shudder rolled through her slight frame. He wanted to pick her up and cart her to the couch, but he managed to restrain that instinct. "Grape juice sounds fantastic," she said. "But I'm not ready to lie down again when I've barely opened my eyes. I'll join you in the kitchen. We can…talk. I'll fill you in how your dogs recued me."

He waited a beat and then another, to see if her body would give in to its obvious weakness. If she sagged to the floor, he could legitimately refuse her offer and insist she rest—without coming off as a Class A jerk—but no. She remained standing, albeit somewhat crookedly propped against the wall, with a hopeful smile. How could she want to talk? If she already wanted to talk, he was done for.

"Tell ya what," he said, swallowing another sigh. "If you can make it to the kitchen without falling, then sure. We can…chat it up while I put together some food."

The second—as in the *very* second—the words came out of his mouth, Maggie pulled herself off the floor and went to Goldi's side. Rather, Meredith's side. Standing straight, the woman put her hand on the top of Maggie's head for balance and, with a determined set to her jaw, said, "Lead the way!"

Hrmph. He should've added "on your own" to his prior statement. As in, "If you can make it to the kitchen *on your own* without falling, then sure." Regrettable error, but an understandable one. He was, after all, beyond exhausted.

Nodding sharply, he turned and strode to the kitchen, shoving his concern for a stranger's well-being *and* his grumpy attitude as far down as possible. It wasn't as if he planned on preparing a feast. He'd open a can of soup, which would take all of five minutes, and slap a slice of bread in the toaster. In less than ten minutes, she'd be eating. She couldn't talk his ear off with food in her mouth, and by the time she was done, she should be ready to collapse.

Ten minutes should be a cinch.

In the kitchen, he pulled out one of the chairs and waited for her and Maggie. She entered a minute later, Maggie still by her side with Max following. Yup. Whether he understood why or not, his dogs had declared Goldi—damn it, *Meredith*—to be one of theirs. Perhaps hearing about how they'd rescued her would clue him in as to why. And yeah, he'd like to know the details of how his dogs had brought her to his couch.

How bad could it be? It was her story, since the dogs—amazing as they were—had yet to learn how to speak the English language, so she would do most of the talking. Realizing that all he had to do was cook and listen, maybe nod every now and then, utter an "ah" or an "is that so?" the tension between his shoulder blades relaxed.

"Here," he said, his voice gruffer than he'd intended, "sit down before you keel over." Now, under the bright, overhead light in the kitchen, her pale skin appeared almost translucent. Those dark circles beneath her eyes could've been the result of being on the losing side of a bar fight. "Last thing you need is to cause more damage to yourself. I'll get you that juice."

Lips stretched into a faint smile as she lowered herself to the chair. "That would be fantastic. And I'm okay. A little weak, yes, but really, not so bad considering."

She was probably the type of person who refused to admit when she was sick, too. He supposed he couldn't give her grief over that, at least not if his sister was anywhere close to hearing distance. He didn't get sick. Or so he told Fiona whenever she tried to coddle him over a cold or what-have-you. He didn't need coddling. Despised coddling.

After handing her the juice, he said, "Drink it nice and slow. There's a lot of sugar in that, and it is ice cold. I guarantee if you chug it down, no matter how thirsty you feel, you will throw up all over my floor, and I don't really feel like cleaning that up."

She nodded and took a grateful sip. "How is it that…" she trailed off. At his confused expression, she said, "Sorry. I forgot to speak my words and just thought the rest of the question. Let me try again…how is it that you have electricity? I mean, with the weather like it is, and that wind, and being so deep in the mountains, I would've guessed you'd have lost power ages ago."

"We did. Or I did." Opening the pantry, he grabbed a can of chicken noodle soup and the loaf of bread. "Yesterday, actually. Not long after I came home and found you."

"Oh." Turning her head, she glanced out the window, at the still-raging storm. "They already got the power back on? In this?"

"Nope." He opened a drawer and retrieved the can opener. "They can't do anything while it's still snowing like that, and even if the snow stopped now, it will take days—if not a week—for the power to be reestablished. I'm used to it, though admittedly, not this early in the season."

"You have power," she said. "Unless I am imagining the lights and the heat, which would mean that I really am delusional."

"I'd say the delusional part remains to be seen, but your observation skills are not in question. Yes, I have power."

She snickered, showing she had a functioning sense of humor. "How?"

"Magic," he said, surprising himself.

"Magic?"

"Yup. You, my dear, were lucky enough to become snowbound with a wizard." Now, where had that come from? Liam wasn't the teasing sort. Never had been, anyway. It didn't feel awful. Actually, he somewhat liked this moment. Dumping the can of soup into a saucepan, he turned the burner on low. "Why do you think I choose to live up here, alone and in complete seclusion? People, even in today's world, tend to become fearful of what they don't understand."

"Afraid you'll be burned at the stake?"

"Nah. I'm a wizard, not a witch."

"Doesn't really matter what you call yourself, if you have magic and people are afraid of magic," she said in a dry manner. "I rather like the idea of it, myself."

"You do, huh?"

"Sure. Why wouldn't I? Magic could ease so many discomforts in life." She took another careful sip of her juice. No puking yet, thank goodness. "And I would be willing to buy into the implausible tale you tell, except for one small detail that has left me confused."

"And that would be?"

She grinned and wrinkled her nose. It was…well, the word *adorable* came to mind. "I don't quite understand how you are able to use magic for electricity, yet…you're heating up a can of soup and toasting bread the old-fashioned way. Why not just wave your hand and have a bowl of homemade soup appear? Along with…hmm, a basket filled with artisan breads?"

"Simple. I didn't say I was a good wizard. Electricity is one thing, but food is quite another. Food takes a lot more skill than turning on the lights. Magically speaking."

"Is that so?" Her lips twitched again. Yup. Adorable. "I would think it would be quite the opposite."

"You would, huh? I agree, but alas, the world of magic isn't based in logic." He felt himself smiling. Whoa. He must be on the edge of collapse if this conversation was amusing him, rather than annoying him. Stirring the soup, he said, "But consider everything that goes into a bowl of soup. It's really quite difficult."

"Huh. I guess that makes a weird sort of sense." Again, she sipped her juice. He was pleased she didn't appear to be having problems with it. "Oh," she said, "I got it. A generator?"

"Yeah. Up here, you pretty much need one." The soup was hot and the toast was done and thanks to his out-of-character whimsy, he'd done all of the talking. Quickly, he buttered the toast and ladled the soup into two over-size mugs, grabbed a couple of spoons and napkins. "Here you go," he said as he set her food in front of her. "Eat up. But…slowly."

"Is that your advice for everything? Go slowly?"

"For a woman who has just gone through what you have? Yup."

"I'm actually doing…okay."

"Good." He sat down across from her and waited for the dogs to sidle next to him, as they did whenever he ate. They didn't. They stayed planted at Goldi's feet, looking up at her with what could only be described as utter devotion.

He knew that look. He'd seen it on his own face a grand total of once. A little over a decade ago, which seemed unbelievable. So much time had passed. An entire lifetime, plus one or two more.

But he hadn't forgotten that look. His dogs were besotted.

"Tell me the story," he said, "of how you met Max and Maggie."

Sky-blue eyes widened in shock. She dropped her spoon, which clattered on the table and sent sprays of broth, along with a few noodles and chunks of chicken, flying into the air. Blinking, she asked, "How I met who?"

"Max and Maggie," he said. She blinked again, obviously still confused. "My dogs? You were going to tell me how they found you, rescued you?"

"Max and Maggie are your dogs! Right. Of course."

"Are you okay? Feeling dizzy or sick to your stomach?" he asked. "We can put this off until later, after we've both slept some."

"No, no. Not that. I just didn't know the dogs' names, so it took a minute for the pieces to connect." Her words came out in a jumble, one on top of another, and a smattering of pink blossomed on her cheeks. "You are correct, though! I promised you the story, and really, it won't take that long to tell."

"If you're sure, then go ahead."

"Yes, I am," she said as she sopped up the soup spill with her napkin. "I'm supposed to be on…vacation. I'm from San Francisco, and I have a friend who lives in Steamboat Springs. Rachel. Who is probably frantic with worry right about now. The last time we spoke was right after my plane landed. I checked in, told her I'd be there soon, and then the storm hit. I got lost."

"She probably is worried, but there isn't anything we can do about that just yet. Once we have phone service again, you can call her." She nodded, but didn't speak.

He waited a few more seconds before saying, "Go on. Eat as you talk. Your body needs the nourishment."

Dragging in a deep breath, she nodded again and started to talk. Bit by bit, as she slowly ate her soup and toast, drank her juice, the entire story came out. With each word spoken, he easily heard the remnants of fear, desperation, loneliness in her voice. Saw it in her eyes, whenever she looked in his direction, and in her body, as she shivered in remembrance.

He felt for her, deeply. In a manner that held zero logic. She wasn't a part of his life. Could not be described as either family or friend. That he knew her at all boiled down to a simple coincidence of timing and location. Yet, he *felt* for her, and had the inane wish that he could step backward in time and meet her at the airport, warn her…lead her in the correct direction, so she'd never have to go through what she had.

So she could escape this haunting fear, stark loneliness and sheer desperation that would likely forever live in her memory.

It would take more effort than she realized at this moment to find peace and acceptance for what had occurred, for all she'd experienced. He knew this with absolute fact. Hell, it had taken him close to five years to free his soul, his heart, from his darkest memory. Some days, he still struggled more than he thought he should, even now, even after almost a decade.

Well, perhaps that right there was the foundation, the reason…the *logic* of feeling so much for a stranger. It was based on pure compassion for another human being's struggle that, while vastly different in the actual facts from his most personal battle, held enough emotional nuances to strike a chord.

Demons. They looked alike, felt alike, despite their origin.

Liam pushed out a breath, set the past aside and focused on this minute with this woman. No matter the reason, he was damn glad his dogs had found her and brought her here, to him. Was glad the coincidence of timing and location had led to her arriving when he was actually in the state and not off on assignment. Was glad he hadn't chosen to stay at his sister's place for the duration of the storm. He was just…glad.

And he didn't need to decipher all the reasons why.

"That had to be absolutely terrifying," he said when she'd finished speaking, when he'd finished thinking. "Draining. But you persevered. You didn't give up and now, you're safe. In another day or two, you'll feel more yourself. And you will know, for the rest of your life, that you are formed of steel. Don't forget that part. Steel. Many people never gain that knowledge."

"Maybe. But really, without your dogs, I don't know how much longer I would've made it." She shrugged as if attempting to lighten her words. Or maybe the fatalistic meaning behind them? Could be either, he supposed. Half collapsing in her chair, she reached one hand down to pat Max's head and said, "I've decided that your dogs are my guardian angels. They saved me."

"You were working on rescuing yourself before they found you. Don't forget that, Meredith." Points to him for speaking her actual name. "Yes, they led you here, but don't minimize your part in saving your own hide. Okay?"

"Okay. Right. I won't. But I can also be ever grateful for Max and Maggie's abilities. They're incredible," she said, smiling. "They're also gorgeous, sort of like a cross between a German shepherd and a fox. What breed are they?"

"You won't get an argument from me on their abilities or their looks," he said. "But to answer your question, they're Belgian Tervurens, herding dogs, and incredibly smart. There isn't a lot they can't do when they set their minds to it, but they've never had the opportunity to rescue a damsel in distress before."

He almost told her about the time, when they were puppies, they managed to open a sealed container of frosted sugar cookies Fiona had baked, without so much as leaving a bite mark on the lid. He'd been outside, had returned to find an empty container and the pups snoozing by the fire. Hell, he hadn't eaten even one of those cookies. And even though he did not have a sweet tooth, they'd looked delicious.

He chose to keep his mouth shut. Yes, he felt for this woman, was relieved she was safe and sound, but he wasn't the type to swap stories. Even about his beloved dogs.

Besides which, she was seriously starting to droop. He guessed she wouldn't be able to keep those blue eyes open that much longer. And hallelujah, when she slept, he'd sleep. *Finally.* His bed was calling to him something fierce.

"Who is who?" she asked over another spoonful of soup. "I'd hate to call Max by Maggie's name or vice versa. Miracle dogs should be correctly identified!"

Miracle dogs, eh? He sort of liked that description. "Maggie is a little shorter than Max, and her coloring is lighter. Less russet and black, more tawny and chestnut. And," he said, feeling a mite foolish, "if you watch them move, Maggie is more graceful. Softer in her gait, though no less agile. Max is brute strength, through and through."

Scooting out her chair a few inches, Meredith leaned over and patted the dogs on their heads. "It is very nice to finally have a proper introduction. Thank you for saving me."

Those words, as few as they were, held the power of a sledgehammer against a marshmallow. His heart being the friggin' marshmallow. He shook off the ludicrous image and focused on the brass tacks. Most of her soup was gone, about half of her toast and she'd drained her juice. Good. "How are you doing?" he asked. "Had enough to eat?"

"Yes," she said, sitting straight. "Plenty. Thank you."

"Welcome." Only one item remained on the list. "Think you have enough energy for a shower? I don't have a bathtub, but if you're worried about standing that long, the shower's big enough for a stool. Can move one in there easy. Don't want you fainting or anything."

The pink returned to her cheeks, darker than before. "A shower is exactly what I need. Thank you," she said with a cute-as-a-button lift to her chin, "but I am fairly sure I can handle standing without passing out. What about my clothes? Are they dry?"

"Dry, yes, but not washed yet." Standing, Liam gathered the dishes and cups. "I'll loan you something else of mine until we get yours taken care of."

"Okay. Yes. Thank you."

Suddenly aggravated and not knowing why, Liam dumped the dishes in the sink, to be cleaned later. "Come on, then. Let's get you situated so you can rest. Once you're settled, I plan on doing the same."

She didn't object or thank him again, just nodded.

Together, with the dogs glued to her side, they left the kitchen.

He brought her another pair of drawstring pajama bottoms, along with a sweatshirt and fresh socks, showed her where the towels were and when she closed the door to the bathroom, he breathed in relief. Now that she was out of his sight, his aggravation lessened.

She didn't seem crazy and hadn't mentioned her strange dreams about him again. In fact, she seemed nice and smart, grateful and easygoing, with a good dash of quirky humor embedded in her personality. He might, though it was much too soon to say, actually like her.

Just that fast, his sour mood returned.

Oh, no. Nope. He didn't want to like her. He didn't want to get to know her any better than he already did. All he wanted was for the damn snow to stop falling, the wind to cease blowing and the roads to clear. So he could go back to his solitary lifestyle.

The life he'd chosen.

Closing her eyes, relishing the feel of being clean and warm and fed, Meredith snuggled under the blanket on the sofa. Liam had gallantly waited for her to shower—and yes, she'd managed to keep standing, barely—and had brought her another glass of juice before taking the stairs to where she assumed his bedroom was. He'd stopped at the top of the stairs, turned around and somewhat sheepishly offered her the use of his bed, saying he could take the couch.

A sweet offer, but no. She didn't think her legs were strong enough for the stairs, and frankly, she preferred this room, this sofa, where she had dreamed a life that she'd adored. If she had any hope of falling back into her dream, she figured she had the best chance of it happening here. And she did want to dream again.

The sound of rumbling footsteps on the stairs forced her eyes open. Max and Maggie, not Liam. Dogs, not children.

Easily explained. She must have heard him call them by name while she slept, even if she didn't recall doing so. Weird, how her brain had taken that scrap of information and turned these two amazing dogs into her children. *Their* children.

Interesting, but really of little consequence. She'd had a dream. A wonderful dream, yes, and one she very much hoped she would have again, but she didn't fool herself into thinking the dream itself meant anything. Now that she was fully awake and able to think logically.

Her guardian angels padded to the side of the couch and whined.

"Come on," she said, "there's plenty of room, as you both well know. Though, I kind of think even if there wasn't enough room, you'd find a way to fit anyway."

Within seconds, both were tucked tight around her body. Max laid his head on her hip and instantly fell asleep. Maggie wrapped herself in a curve at Meredith's feet and did the same. And never, in her entire life, had she felt quite so secure. So…at peace with herself and her surroundings. How was that?

Why was that? She should be uncomfortable, frantic for the storm to end so she could contact Rachel, let her know that she was alive and continue with what she had originally planned. She should be desperate to touch base with her parents, because despite everything else, they remained her family. She should feel awkward in this house, hidden away with a man she did not know, like any other normal woman would. She should feel…

pensive and concerned for her well-being. She should feel a million and one ways that she did not, in any manner whatsoever, feel.

That, too, probably fell firmly on the inconsequential side of things.

Rather than dwell on how she didn't feel, Meredith chose to focus on the truths of her situation. And right now, those facts were pretty darn awesome. She was alive. And yes, she was clean, warm and fed. She was safe. And even without her dream as a backdrop, she couldn't deny that Liam, the real man and not the imaginary one, fully intrigued her.

Yes, he intrigued her…with his quiet, bordering-on-brusque attitude one second, and then stating he was a wizard in that firm, no-argument tone, with the slightest lift to the corners of his mouth the next. With the love he obviously felt for his dogs and how he'd cared for her, a stranger. The concern he showed. His constant "take it slow" advice, and…and *oh*.

The way he'd looked at her as she'd told him her story, with intensity and interest, almost as if he could see straight into her soul…well, that was something new. Yet another first.

In addition to all of that, she believed, regardless of how little sense the believing made, that she was here with this particular man at this particular time because she was supposed to be. Not because of her dream or the fantasy her brain had concocted, but due to where she was at in her life and the uniqueness, the suddenness of this situation.

She had walked—no, make that *stumbled*—into Liam's life for a reason. It had to be a good reason.

Probably not the lifetime of love she'd dreamed about, but something worthwhile. Something positive and fulfilling and valid. Something that maybe, just maybe, both she and Liam had been lacking their entire lives thus far. Something they might learn from each other, that they wouldn't be able to learn any other way.

It was a good thought.

And if it was correct, she couldn't wait to see what that something turned out to be, to discover the precise reason that fate had tossed her into a series of cataclysmic events only to end up precisely *here*.

For now, though, she chose to sleep. To regain more energy. Because she had a feeling that Liam the wizard was sure to keep her on her toes, for however long her "visit" lasted. Hopefully, this storm would rage for... weeks.

Chapter Five

Music? Liam opened his dry, scratchy eyes and sat up in bed, instantly on the alert. His mind thick from sleep, he tried to make sense of what he heard. Why was music— ABBA, he thought—blasting through his house? Strike that. *Blasting* was an inaccurate description, as the volume wasn't quite that loud, but there shouldn't be any music. He lived alone. Unless his dogs had figured out how to—oh. *Goldi.* "Meredith," he mumbled, tossing off his blankets.

He threw on a T-shirt and looked outside the window. Snowing. Still. Though, not quite as violently as before he fell asleep. Or perhaps that was only wishful thinking. Next, he picked up his watch—which had once belonged to his father—and frowned.

Eight o'clock? Morning, based on the hazy light suffusing his room and the fact that he could see more than two feet outside of his window, so he'd slept...twelve hours? Twice his typical amount? Well, hell.

He hadn't done that in almost ten years. In the days after the tragedy that had forever changed his life, that for too long had filled him with regret.

He'd fallen in love in a whirlwind romance, had proposed and within a year was married and expecting his first child. They'd only known each other three months before they tied the knot, six before she had gotten pregnant.

Sure, he'd had his concerns and she'd had hers, but they were in love and believed that was enough to buffer them through any storm. They were wrong.

Home base was in Denver then, since that was where Christy had been born and raised, where her family lived. Seemed only fair to keep her in familiar surroundings where she had support, since his job took him out of the country so often. They lived in a typical house in a typical neighborhood, with too many people for Liam's comfort, but for Christy...well, he'd put up with just about anything. Even living in the middle of suburbia.

She'd been almost seven months pregnant when he'd gone to parts of the Amazon Basin to photograph birds for *National Geographic*.

It was a long assignment—six weeks—and Christy hadn't wanted him to go. She'd almost pleaded with him to stay, but he'd convinced her that by accepting the job, he'd be able to pass on any other assignments for a good long while afterward. So that he'd be close at hand for their baby's birth and through the first year.

That had been the plan. Privately, he'd hated the idea of turning down the opportunity, because he figured it would be the last extended assignment he'd take for... well, years.

After some discussion, Christy had agreed. Of course she had. She was a sweetheart and tended to look after his needs more often than her own, and she'd seen the logic in his argument.

The morning he left, he'd kissed her and her baby belly, promised to touch base as regularly as he could, reminded her of how very much he loved her and he... walked out of their house. When he'd returned four weeks later, rather than six, it was to bury his wife and unborn child.

Carbon-monoxide poisoning had stolen them away while she slept, while he was thousands of miles away taking photographs of birds.

Didn't matter what he knew—that it wasn't his fault, and if he'd been at home, he would've been sleeping right beside her. The guilt had nearly consumed him, the loss had nearly destroyed him.

It had taken far too much time to locate stable ground once again. To find any peace within himself and, eventually, forgiveness. This house, the mountains, his career, his solitary existence—save for his sister and niece and his dogs—had, bit by bit, returned him to a state of near normalcy. He was better now, for the most part. Scarred, sure. How could he not be? But time did have a way with healing whatever wounds it could, and those that couldn't be healed...well, they hardened and quit hurting so damn much. So a man could breathe, accept and carry on.

Liam forcibly shook himself out of his memories, shoved the entirety of that particular past into the recesses of his mind and took the stairs two at a time.

Where were Max and Maggie? Not with him, as they normally were. They would need to go out. They needed to be fed. And he'd have to deal with this woman who, for whatever reason, thought it was appropriate to listen to "Mamma Mia" at a higher-than-reasonable volume in a stranger's house, while that stranger slept, at eight in the freaking morning.

A stranger who'd saved her butt, no less.

Nope, his inner Jiminy Cricket proclaimed, *your dogs saved her butt, you just…ah, warmed it up some, along with the rest of her body.* True story there, but these facts did not alter Liam's annoyance one iota. *His* house. *His* part of the mountain.

He should be able to sleep all damn day if he chose, without worry that some woman and her love of a Swedish pop group would wake him from a near-dead sleep. It was, at the very least, inconsiderate. Bordering on rude. And something that required discussion, now, so that it did not happen again for however long he was stuck in these walls with Miss Goldilocks.

Moving through the living room, he noted that she'd folded the blankets on the sofa into a nice, neat pile, and that she'd fed the fire at some point, so that it still burned warmly, gently. That was decent of her, thoughtful.

This realization, however, did not cool his frustration. Here, the music was louder, more annoying and the last damn thing he wanted to hear. He wanted quiet. Silence. He wanted the normalcy of returning home from assignment and not having to deal with another human being until he was good and ready.

At the entrance to the kitchen, he stopped. Bubbling annoyance melted into a pool of nothingness as he stared.

The small oak table, which his grandfather had made with his own hands, was set for two. The dishes from last night were washed and drying in the stainless steel counter rack. And Goldi was standing in front of the stove, whipping up what looked to be a breakfast for a king. Eggs. Bacon. Pancakes.

And as she cooked, her hips swayed to the beat of the music, and her mane of curly blond hair all but bounced on her shoulders.

His dogs…his *traitorous* dogs…were sitting on their haunches near the door to the mudroom, watching Goldi with that adoring gaze. Of course, she was frying a panful of bacon. That could account for the love pouring from their eyes.

But he didn't think so. Based on the quickening of his pulse and the tightening in his gut just at the very sight of this woman, he couldn't really blame them, either. She had a way. A way that tended to appeal just as much, if not more, than frustrate. And they'd barely spent any time awake together. Didn't seem to bode well for him.

"Morning," he said, his tone sounding rough to his own ears. "You seem to be feeling…ah, let's go with spirited. Slept well, did you?"

"Yes, Yoda, I slept quite well, and before you ask…I am feeling much better today," she said, turning on her heel to face him. A quirky, almost mischievous grin lifted her lips. She reached over and picked up her phone, which she'd plugged into an outlet, slid her finger across the screen and the music stopped. Blissful silence filled the room. "Hungry? I hope so, because I seem to have gone a bit overboard here."

With those simply stated words, his inner grouch quit fighting to resurface and disappeared into the nether, smothered by another person's—this specific person's— kindness.

Nope, he wasn't hungry. Liam rarely ate breakfast, but no way and no how was he prepared to dim the glow in Meredith's beautiful blue eyes. Today, he didn't see any of the fear or loneliness he'd witnessed last night.

"Starving," he said, rubbing his stomach for emphasis. "And preparing breakfast was unnecessary, but thank you. I'm unaccustomed to people cooking my meals. Unless I am at my sister's place for dinner or I have to eat at a restaurant. It's very thoughtful of you, and…well, very much appreciated."

"I like to cook," she said simply. "Can't do a lot else for you at the moment, so…"

Her words trailed off, she shrugged and returned her focus to the stove. The silence went from blissful to a heavy type of awkwardness. Why?

Frowning, unable to think of anything else to say but needing to say something, he went with, "Looks as if breakfast is about ready. I'll let the dogs out. If there's anything I can do to help when I get back, I'll—"

"Oh! No need," she said over her shoulder. "I let them out earlier. We had to go through the front door. The snowdrifts in the back are piled ridiculously high. They did their thing and came right back in without any trouble. It's nasty out there."

"Okay, then. Thank you." There went that idea. And he doubted that he'd ever expressed his thanks so often in so short of a time in his entire life. "I'll just get them fed, so they're not begging at the table while we eat. After breakfast, I'll clear some of that snow in the back before it gets any higher. It looks as if we might be nearing the tail end of the storm."

Thank God.

"Tail end, huh?"

"Think so. Hope so." He stepped fully into the kitchen and whistled to the dogs. Both snapped their gazes to his for all of half a second. "Bet you two are hungry, huh?"

"I actually fed them, too." Goldi tossed him an apologetic look before flipping two pancakes onto a plate and pouring another large spoonful of batter into the pan.

"I wasn't sure if that would be okay, since I don't know their schedule, but they were adamant."

Straightened the living room, added logs to the fire, took care of his dogs and was in the process of making him breakfast. Twenty-four hours ago, this woman lay unconscious on his couch and here she stood, apparently with every last thing under control. "Thank you," he repeated, instantly wincing. "I'm all yours, then. Anything you need help with?"

"Coffee, I guess? I meant to start that earlier."

Coffee! Hell yes. Caffeine was his ambrosia. Caffeine should jumpstart his brain, so he could think and regain control. Because right now, his world was spinning off its axis and he didn't know how to stop the spinning. "I can do that. Not a problem."

He grabbed the bag of coffee from the freezer and tried—oh, how he tried—to pretend that his entire being wasn't centered on the tiny blonde in front of his stove. Or how adorable she looked wearing his navy plaid pajama bottoms—far too large for her small frame and rolled up at the ankles so she wouldn't trip—and his forest green sweatshirt that just about hung to her knees.

Her curves were well hidden by the oversize clothing, and frankly there shouldn't be one damn thing about her current appearance that could account for the tight ball of heat in the pit of his stomach. But she appealed to him, nonetheless. Made him want what he hadn't wanted in… forever. Caused sweat to form on the back of his neck.

Sweat! How could she do that?

All of this was uncomfortable. Jarring. And a state of affairs he needed to get under control. Fast. But Lord, she made it difficult. Not only due to his nonsensical attraction, but…well, damn it all, she *fit* somehow.

In the way she jockeyed around him while he filled the

pot with water, reached in front of him for a plate she'd left on the counter, tossed him a grin when they went for the dishtowel at the same time. It—*this*—felt familiar. It resonated. Her being here seemed easy, comfortable and…like the normal way of things.

Except, of course, none of this was normal. Distance was called for. Walls required building. *Rules* needed to be set. Because whatever was happening here couldn't be allowed to continue. He'd traveled the yellow-brick road of following his heart instead of his common sense before, and that had not turned out well by *anyone's* standards. He would not err again.

He was a man meant to be on his own. He did not need to be taught that lesson again.

"Once we're done with breakfast, I'll spend a couple hours outside, clearing the snow around the back door and shoveling a path to the shed. I need to check the generator, make sure we're good still. And then, well, then I need to get some work done." He said all of this lightning fast, in a no-room-for-argument tone, just as the coffee started to brew. "You're welcome to make yourself at home. Feel free to poke around and do whatever you want to pass the time, but I will be busy. All day. Sorry about that, but a storm doesn't negate my responsibilities."

"Oh. I see. Okay. And of course it doesn't." Disappointment rang in her words, which made him feel like a heel, but he didn't backtrack.

She transferred the bacon—what appeared to be an entire pound, perfectly cooked—to a plate. Then, with the skillet of scrambled eggs in hand, she dished them each a serving at the table and asked, "You work at home, I take it?"

His mule-headed nature kicked in, fierce. A normal

question to ask, but he refused to be dragged into a conversation he did not want to have. General conversation? No problem. But anything deeper seemed a very bad idea, considering the current set of circumstances. He couldn't outright ignore her question, either. *That* would be rude. He went with, "Partially."

"Let me guess," she said, her teasing humor returning. "Donning your wizard hat and casting spells? What is on today's agenda, creating havoc or harmony or something in between?"

He liked her. Damn it. He *liked* her. "Perhaps a little of both."

"Hmm. Well, if you could use your sorcery to get the phones working, even for a few minutes, that would be very much appreciated. I keep thinking about Rachel and how worried she must be. And if she contacted my family, they'll also be worried." She flinched and her chin lifted. "I mean, I think they'd be worried. They'll probably be worried."

Think? What kind of family did she have that she couldn't state with unequivocal certainty that they would be worried? There was a story there, and yup, he was curious.

But he kept his questions to himself. Even so, her statement bothered him. That it did managed to bother him more. The fact she had the power to bounce his thoughts around like a basketball bothered him the most. He did not know her. She meant nothing to him. Yet, here they were.

"Wish I could do that for you," he said about the phones. "But as we surmised last night, I'm not a wizard. The most I can do is get you out of here the second the weather and the roads allow. Besides which, chances are high that your friend doesn't have phone service, either. Or power."

"Right. Of course. I was just teasing. And I figured I'd call her mobile, but who knows. I should quit worrying. I'll contact her when I can, as soon as I can."

"I know you were teasing, and somehow I doubt you'll stop worrying. But," he said, "give it a shot. Worrying won't solve a damn thing."

Neither spoke for a few seconds, but then, as she set the plate of pancakes and the syrup bottle on the table, she asked, "So you're not a wizard. What are you then? A butcher, baker or candlestick maker? King of some country I've never heard of?"

He grinned. He couldn't help himself, and the answer slipped out. "Photographer."

"What type? Wedding, babies, families…that sort of thing?"

Flinching at the idea of being around so many people so often, especially crying babies, he asked, "Since when did we start playing a game of twenty questions?" He retrieved two extra-large coffee mugs from the cupboard. "How do you take your coffee?"

"No sugar. Cream if you have it, but if you don't, milk is good. And we might as well get to know each other a little since we're cooped up together. Don't you think?"

"Ah." No, he did not think. Yet, he couldn't say so without hurting her feelings. A thought he despised. "I guess that makes sense."

"So…what type of photographer?"

"The type that uses cameras." She was a persistent one, he'd give her that. Well, he could be more so. "I have the powdered version of cream…want that or prefer the milk?"

"Powdered is fine." She tapped her sock-covered foot

in mock impatience. Or he thought so, anyway. "I'm waiting. Who do you photograph? Babies, families, brides and grooms, or...?"

"Wildlife, mostly." He filled the mugs with coffee, preparing hers as she'd asked. And that, too, felt familiar. Normal and comfortable, even if the questions weren't. More so than he often felt when Fiona and Cassie were visiting, and they were his family. Now that was something that *didn't* make a lick of sense. He hated when he couldn't logic out a solution. "What about you? Butcher, baker or candlestick maker?"

Once breakfast was done, he'd make darn sure he stayed far away from Goldi until she was, hopefully, conked out on the sofa tonight. With his dogs, since they now seemed to prefer her over him. He couldn't fault them for their good taste.

"At the moment, I am in between jobs. But I worked as a stager for several years." She sat down at the table in the same chair she used the night before. "I liked it. Quite a bit, actually, but your job sounds so much more interesting. What type of wildlife?"

"Any type. All types." He wasn't quite sure what a stager was, but didn't much feel like asking, so he didn't.

Sitting down at the table, he took a large gulp of his coffee. He had to admit that the spread on the table was impressive, in sight and smell. His stomach rumbled in response, which shocked him. Typically, he didn't get hungry until lunch. "Everything looks amazing."

"Well, enjoy." She served herself a pancake and a few strips of bacon. "I'm a master in the kitchen at breakfast, but that's the extent of my culinary knowledge. Other than sandwiches."

"Nothing wrong with a good sandwich," he managed to say.

"No, I guess there isn't." Darting her gaze downward, she concentrated on her food, on slowly and methodically taking one bite at a time.

Following her lead, he filled his plate and tried to ignore the guilt gnawing his gut to shreds.

It was *not* his job to entertain this woman. She was his guest, but only by…well, force seemed too harsh a word, but it wasn't far off. And worse, much worse, he didn't feel himself around her, which further complicated the situation. What he wanted was for them to exist in their separate corners until she could leave, in order to preserve his sanity.

There were a few problems there. His place wasn't tiny, but it wasn't built for two people to stay out of each other's way. It seemed selfish. Mostly, though, he didn't want her to feel bad.

He'd go for some honesty, see where that took them. "I'm sorry," he said. "I can see you're trying here, and I appreciate your intent. I really do. I'm just not much of a socializer."

"It's okay," she said, her voice quiet. She looked at him and smiled. "Really. I get it. You wish I wasn't here. You're used to being by yourself, and in from the storm, here I am, and now you're stuck with me. I'm sorry about that, and I'll try to be less…sociable."

Lie through his teeth or go for more honesty? Liam pushed his eggs around on his plate before choosing the careful answer of, "It isn't that I wish you were gone. Don't think that. I'm glad you're here, relieved my dogs found you and brought you to safety. But you're not wrong in everything else you said. I am not a people person, by anyone's definition."

"So you're the guy at parties who hides in the corner, sipping his drink, hoping no one talks to you and watching the clock, waiting for the polite time to leave."

"Nope. I'm the guy who doesn't go to parties. Or barbecues or picnics or family reunions, unless I have absolutely no other choice. If I could figure out how, I wouldn't even go to the grocery store," he said. "Unfortunately, I've yet to train the dogs to shop for me."

"I bet they could learn," she said with a laugh. "And this might surprise you, but I'm not a people person, either. I can force it, though. Most people who meet me think I'm an extrovert, when the complete opposite is the truth. I tend to need lots of time after expending that type of energy to regroup, to find my bearings again, so I really do get it."

"You have one up on me. I barely get by in any social situation. Usually, when I'm forced to attend one," he said, surprised at his willingness to share even this, "I stand there, trying to find the right thing to say and counting the seconds until I can make my escape. I've always been that way."

Well, in most circumstances. He didn't feel that way with his sister or a few of his longtime friends or when the topic of conversation surrounded an area of interest. He could talk about photography and some of his favorite locales around the world forever.

Tipping her chin, so their eyes met, she nodded. "I hate that feeling. You wish the floor would open up and suck you away. My family attended a lot of social occasions when I was growing up, and I used to hate them. But my dad taught me a trick that made it easier."

"Oh, yeah?" He might just be able to stare into this woman's eyes for hours on end. They called to him, somehow. Soothed him. Made him feel…enough. "What would that be?"

"When you don't know what to say to another person, ask them a question. Any question. Doesn't much matter what it is because the attention is diverted back to them, and all you have to do is listen…and then ask another question based on whatever they said." She shrugged. "You can even avoid answering their questions that way. Just keep asking your own."

Was that why she'd been asking him so many questions? "That works for you, huh?"

She picked up a slice of bacon, broke it in half and gave a piece to each of his dogs, who were on their haunches right next to her chair. Maggie licked her palm. Lucky dog. "It really does. With most people." She shot him a grin. "Try it…ask me a question. Anything at all."

Giving in to her charm, her rather easygoing nature, her innate appeal, he nodded. "Oh, all right. What is a stager? I have the impression it does not involve an actual stage in a theater."

"No, it doesn't, but wouldn't that be fun? And that is a great question." Another piece of bacon, which she split in half and again fed to the dogs. He should tell her that was enough, as he didn't give Max and Maggie table food all that often, but hey…bacon wasn't going to hurt them. "I staged houses to look their best, keeping in mind the area and the targeted pool of buyers, to make them more appealing, so they'd sell fast and hopefully at top dollar."

"Furniture, artwork, knickknacks, that sort of thing?"

"That's it, exactly. If there were special architectural details or an interesting design element to a room, I'd play that up. The goal," she said, popping a bite of bacon into her mouth, "was for a buyer to walk into the home and think, 'I could live here. I want to live here.'"

"Were you good at it?"

"I think so. I enjoyed the creative elements of the job.

I loved conceptualizing how a room should look and then putting all the pieces together to achieve that vision."

He nodded. "I can see how that would be rewarding."

Silence kicked into being once again, which he filled by eating a few forkfuls of his eggs. No longer feeling the consuming need to finish eating and make his escape, but disliking the quiet, Liam took Goldi's advice and asked another question. "How did you meet Rachel if she lives here and you live in San Francisco?"

"Through some of those various social events I mentioned earlier. Rachel grew up in New York, but over the years, we were at the same place at the same time often enough, and we're the same age." Goldi shrugged. "I guess it was natural we became friends."

She hadn't said much, but Liam was struck with the image of two young girls stuck in places they didn't want to be, had found each other and a bond formed. "Tell me about the first time you met. How old were you? What was the social event?"

Long lashes blinked. "You're getting pretty good at this question thing."

"I'm a fast learner. Or," he said with a grin, "maybe you're a great teacher."

Cupping her coffee mug in her hands, she said, "Either or both. But to answer, we were twelve. Our fathers are both businessmen, so even though they don't work directly with each other, they have numerous connections. I met Rachel in the lobby of a hotel." A quick grin flitted across her face. "We were at a charity fund raiser. It involved dinner and endless speeches, and it was one of those things where our fathers wanted to show off their families. We both sneaked away out of sheer boredom, bumped into each other and…I don't know, we just clicked."

There were so many more questions he could ask, but eventually, she'd volley a few his way. Since she'd answered his, he'd have to answer hers, which would open another entire field of curiosity on both sides. They could be stuck at this table for hours.

Not an entirely distasteful thought. Perhaps even an enjoyable one, depending on where their conversation led. The danger existed in the possibility of exposing areas of himself he just did not talk about. With anyone. Even a charming blonde with beautiful blue eyes.

"I'm glad you two met," he said, putting an end to the questions. "My guess is the rest of that night was much more enjoyable for the both of you."

"Oh, it was. As were any of the functions we attended together after that. For a while, I even hoped she'd manage to fall in love with one of my brothers, so we could be sisters."

"Brothers? How many? Older or younger?" Damn it. There he went, asking more questions. Giving into his curiosity when he should be outside, clearing a path and making sure everything was in order. "It's okay, you don't have to—"

"Two. Both older. Both married now, with kids." She finished eating the last of her pancake before asking, "You mentioned a sister. Is she your only sibling?"

"Yup." Standing before he asked something else, he started clearing off the table. "You cooked, so I'll clean. Shower if you want, and there are a ton of books in the living room. A few decks of playing cards, too, if you like solitaire. Make yourself at home."

"Sure," she said. "I appreciate that! We'll get done quicker in here if I help, though."

"It isn't necessary. I can take care of this."

"I know. I'd like to help. Besides which," she said,

filling the sink with soapy water, "you've already stated you'll be busy for the entire day. I have plenty of time to shower, look through your books and play solitaire. Or whatever else I can come up with."

He didn't argue further even though he wanted to. It would prove fruitless, and her point held validity. Together, they tidied the kitchen and again, the way they moved around each other seemed effortless. As if they were accustomed to doing so. Comfortable. Easy. *Familiar.*

A state of being that landed squarely in the irrational range.

Chapter Six

Make herself at home, huh? Meredith sighed and thumbed through the books on the shelf for the third time. Liam's selection of books was rather narrowly focused, most of them nonfiction, either about photography, remote locations around the world, different species of animals or—big surprise here—filled with photographs of remote locations around the world and different species of animals.

The handful of novels he owned were, by and large, of the action-and-adventure type. Spies and private detectives and mystery thrillers, none of which appealed. She wanted to lose herself in something light and easy. Frivolous and fun.

Biting her lip, she stared at Liam's closed office door, which was next to the stairs going up to his bedroom.

Earlier, he'd dashed in after clearing some of the snow, took a shower and after a small, tight smile directed at her and a reminder to make herself at home, had disappeared into that room with the dogs. She hadn't seen nor heard from him since.

Which was perfectly fine. It wasn't as if he'd invited her to visit and then had chosen to make himself inaccessible. The guy had a life. Responsibilities. But geez, was she ever bored.

She could, she supposed, play another three dozen rounds of solitaire. Or try to take a nap. Or braid her hair or count to one million or…it was after three o'clock, and she hadn't eaten lunch.

Liam hadn't, either, unless he had a picnic basket tucked away in his office, which she doubted. He'd expended a ton of physical energy dealing with the snow, and now she had to assume he was expending a ton of mental energy. Doing whatever he was doing.

How could it hurt to make him a plate of food, a fresh cup of coffee, leave them outside of his door with a quick knock? She'd walk away so he wouldn't feel forced to talk, and he could get right back to work. And maybe after she ate, she'd fall into a food coma and be able to take that nap. A long one, please, so by the time she woke, there wouldn't be so many hours to fill. Surely, tonight at some point, he'd sit here with her by the fire, and they could talk.

Get to know each other a little more. Get to know *him* a little more.

Making lunch might not be the best plan, but at least it gave her a task in this moment and, really, that was about as positive as it was going to get. And if she couldn't sleep afterward, she'd give in and read one of those spy novels or find another way to spend the next many hours.

In the kitchen, Meredith grilled two ham-and-cheese sandwiches, added a handful of salt-and-vinegar chips and some green grapes to the plate, looked for and didn't find anything dessert-like—not even a single box of cookies—and after giving up on that, poured him a mug of coffee and called the job done. It wasn't much of a meal, but it was sustenance.

A small pad of paper sat on the counter, next to the useless phone. After a small amount of deliberation, she jotted a note that said, "Thought you might be hungry!" and drew a smiley face with a wizard hat.

There. Done. Her stomach sloshed with nerves, which was just silly. Pushing her apprehension to the side, Meredith returned to the living room and quickly placed his lunch and the note on the floor. Rapping on the door once, she turned on her heel and made her escape, feeling very much as if she were involved in a game of Ding Dong Ditch.

Her heart regained its normal rhythm the second she returned to the cozy, comfortable kitchen. She liked this room, liked the simplicity of the decor, the natural wood cupboards and the concrete countertops, the way that everything fit without overtaking the small space.

She took her own plate to the table and sat down, wondering if she'd be able to hear him open the door. She hoped he wouldn't think she was trying to get his attention or time—because, really, she understood their situation, and if he had to work, he had to work. She hoped he'd appreciate the makeshift lunch. She hoped it wouldn't be seen as an intrusion.

She'd already intruded into this man's life enough.

Picking through her meal halfheartedly, she ate most of what she'd served herself before sighing in frustration. Clean up, and then she'd try that nap.

As the kitchen was compact and well organized to begin with, tidying the area took no time at all. And she felt weak more than tired, which pointed to the fact that she probably needed the rest. So, okay. She'd choose a book, snuggle into the sofa with a couple of blankets and read. Maybe she'd sleep.

When she entered the living room, though, and saw Liam's lunch sitting on the floor untouched, unwanted emotion swam to the surface.

Really? He couldn't even be bothered to pick up the damn plate? Or take it to the kitchen and say, "Hey, thanks for this, but I'm not hungry"?

Though, even as she thought the words, they didn't seem to fit the man. Oh, she knew full well they were mostly strangers, but he had tried to talk to her last night and this morning. He'd taken care of her. He had definitely shown concern for her well-being.

Just that fast, her brewing emotions settled. He hadn't heard her knock. He didn't know she'd made him lunch. He was, as his sister called him, a hermit, but he wasn't rude or inconsiderate, so…yes, he just hadn't heard the knock. Well, she'd take care of that.

She walked over, raised her fist to knock and the door opened. Another millisecond and she'd have clocked the poor man on his chest. Startled, she stepped to the side and managed to kick over the rapidly cooling cup of coffee, which—naturally—spilled onto the plate of food.

"Well, hi there," he said with an amused expression. "Whatcha doing?"

"Apparently, I am ruining your lunch." Heat touched her cheeks. Not only due to the circumstances, but due to his physical presence. He only wore a pair of jeans and a T-shirt, but on him, they looked…*he* looked almost too good to be real. "Which I left here for you, and I knocked but…it doesn't actually matter. If you're hungry, I can make you another sandwich. And of course, I'll deal with the mess I just made. Sorry about that."

"You're sorry for making me lunch?" His forehead creased into furrows. "Then why, pray tell, did you go to the trouble? Seems counterproductive."

"No, I'm not sorry I brought you lunch. I'm sorry for spilling coffee all over your floor and ruining your lunch," she explained. He grinned and she realized he was teasing her. She liked this side of him, so she gave some back. "Though, really, I shouldn't be sorry. It's more your fault than mine that it even happened. For opening the door at that precise second."

"Ah, yes. I would have to agree. That was an extraordinarily thoughtless move on my part." Bending at his knees, he picked up the note, read it and grinned again. Her heart sort of did a spinning dive at the sight of that smile. "Love the wizard hat. Nicely done and don't worry about the mess. We agreed it was my fault. I'll take care of it."

"You always insist on doing everything on your own?" The dogs made their appearance then, pushing their bodies around Liam and all but drooling over the coffee-saturated lunch. "Or does that trait only appear with women you find unconscious on your sofa?"

"I don't insist on doing everything on my own," he said. "It's just how I am. And seeing how I live alone, it's good I'm that way. Otherwise, nothing would ever get done."

Well, that was true. But, "Not while I'm here, you don't live alone. And I can't sit around and just wait. I'll be bored out of my skull, so I might as well be helpful. If you'll let me?"

His eyes narrowed, causing them to crinkle at the corners and his jaw hardened. One quick shake of his head and, "Just take it easy while you're here. You went through something extraordinarily difficult, and I... well." He rubbed his free hand over his face. "I don't need help, Meredith, with anything, but I appreciate your offer. And your willingness. Just take it easy, read, relax."

"Making you a meal when I have to make one for myself anyway is not a hardship," she said, raising her chin a notch. She could out-stubborn just about anyone, being the daughter of the most stubborn man alive. "Maybe you don't mean it this way, but when you tell me to 'just take it easy, read, relax,' I hear, 'sit in the corner and be quiet, so I forget you're here.'"

"That is on you, because that is not what I said."

"I would bet that is what you thought, though," she said, lifting her chin another inch. "You said I should make myself at home, correct?"

"Yes."

"Did you mean those words?"

He sighed, ran his hand over his jaw. "Yes."

"Well, then I win. I get to help out, as that is part of the definition of making myself at home." She pointed toward his office. "So you can go back to work and I will take care of this mess and make you a new lunch. Listen for the knock. I'll just leave it out here."

With that, she picked up the plate and the now-empty coffee mug and took off before he could offer more objections. She was about two steps from the kitchen when his deep, rolling laugh hit her ears. It was a good sound, that laugh.

"Stop, Meredith. I'm done with work," he said from behind her. "I was on my way to find you. I thought you might want some company, seeing how I abandoned you for most of the day. And the dogs were whining at the door, probably because they missed you."

"Company would be nice," she said, smiling from ear to ear. Something, fortunately, that Liam could not see since her back was still facing him. Who cared if he made this choice out of guilt? She was lonely. She did want his company. And regardless of the reason, it was still *his* decision. "I missed them, too. Did you have anything in particular in mind, or just want to sit and talk some more? I'd love to—"

"Sit and talk? More?" She heard a sigh and had to swallow a laugh. "Sitting and talking is one idea, I suppose. I was thinking more along the lines of...well, see, I have a few board games for when my sister and niece visit. Monopoly, Scrabble...um, a few others. Can't think what they are right now. Feel up to something like that?"

"Sure. That works." She took a breath and pivoted, so she could see his face. "I'll clean this up and get you something else to eat and I'll be all set. You can choose the game."

"Nope. I'm not all that hungry, and I want you to rest. I'll deal with clean-up." He approached her and removed the dishes from her hands. "No arguing for once, okay?"

Their eyes met and heat flashed, for just a second, between them. On her side, at least. And it felt...good. Reminded her that she was alive. That she wasn't done. That she still had time to follow her dreams, figure out who she was—who she could become—and to open herself to possibilities she never truly had before. She had time. Thanks to this man and his dogs.

Thanks to herself, too. She'd persevered.

"Okay," she said, knowing when she was beat. "I'll take it easy until you're ready to lose at whatever game we play."

"Perfect." He whistled at the dogs. "I'm just going to

let them out and then I'm yours for the night. You should know, though, I rarely lose at Monopoly or Scrabble."

Hers for the night? She liked the sound of that, too. Probably a bit more than she should, but right now a world of possibilities beckoned and she welcomed them all. Especially those that might include this man. He intrigued her. Deeply. And his eyes did something to her soul.

Warmth whooshed through her, from head to toe, and she fought the temptation to fan herself. "Oh, yeah?" she managed to ask. "Well, neither do I."

One eyebrow raised. "Is that so? Is that a challenge, Goldi?"

"Meredith," she corrected instantly, though she didn't know why. She liked that he called her Goldi. "And yes, you can take it that way. So, let out the dogs and…we'll see who wins."

He nodded and whistled at the dogs again, leading them past her and through the kitchen to the back door.

She stood there motionless for another minute, waiting for her skin to cool and her heart to stop racing. Why this man, when there was so very much she didn't know about him? Why now, when her primary goal should be focusing on creating the life she yearned for?

She didn't know the answer to those questions, but she knew one thing for sure: she was done allowing the "should nots" to clutter her brain. They had never done her any good in the past, so it was time to try something different. Something new. Something courageous.

And just…live.

They were, Liam noted, evenly matched. So far, they'd played Monopoly—he'd won—followed by a game of Scrabble—she'd won—and they'd just finished their second round of Crazy Eights, and yup, one win for each. Throughout each game, they'd kept up a steady stream of chatter that stayed solidly within the impersonal range of topics.

Her last name…his. How much longer until the storm ended—by morning, he guessed—and other miscellaneous topics that included his dogs, where she went to college and not much else other than general conversation, a little teasing here and there about whatever game they were in the midst of.

All of this should have relieved Liam to no end, and through the first couple of games, it did. But now, he was dismayed to realize his curiosity was building.

He found he wanted to know more about the woman. About Meredith. Why she wasn't sure if her family would be worried. Why she left a job she'd apparently liked and was good at.

What made her smile? What made her sad? Why did she, every now and then, seem to look at him as if she knew him, knew what was in his head…in his heart? Of course, she didn't. Couldn't, even. But that look seemed to state otherwise and raised his curiosity another notch.

Made him wonder what it would be like to really let someone—particularly her—in. He'd gone down that road before, to a disastrous and heartbreaking result, and he was a fool to revisit the idea. But there it was, front and center in his thoughts.

Did that make him a sucker for punishment? Perhaps. Probably. Or at the very least, proved that he wasn't as content with his life as he'd believed. A sobering realization and not one he wanted to give credence to just yet.

Also, though he'd never verbally admit it, he wondered about that dream she'd had, even though she hadn't mentioned it again. A lot happened in that dream, she had said. And that a meeting had to occur before anything else. What was *anything else*? What exactly had she dreamed?

Asinine to have his thoughts so fully occupied by another person's dream. Especially a person who had gone through what she had in the hours before collapsing. Exhausted. Freezing. Scared. From what she had said, hopeless by the time his dogs had led her to safety.

She'd heard his voice, had maybe caught a glimpse of his face when she'd opened her eyes for that brief second and in her exhaustion and fear, her hopelessness, had a dream about him...*them*? Seemed that way, and he couldn't blame her for that, couldn't call her crazy.

She'd obviously forgotten all about it, so why couldn't he?

It went back to that look, which she happened to be giving him right now, as if she was thinking about her dream if not outright talking about it. Worse, though, as if she could read his friggin' thoughts. He wasn't sure he liked that.

Wasn't altogether sure he didn't like it, either.

"We have to play one more game," he said quickly, both to wipe out her expression and to distract his oddball thoughts. "To determine the...ah, Blizzard Gaming Championship."

She raised an eyebrow and grinned. "What does the winner get?"

"Pride and a boost to their ego?" he said. "Need more than that?"

"Seeing how I am planning on taking that championship, yes, I do." Her voice held a teasing quality, and her eyes were bright. Happy. He liked that. "There needs to be a prize."

"Ah. I could order a trophy. If you win, that is. I'm

happy enough with the title." Shrugging, he put the playing cards back in their respective boxes. "As big and ostentatious a trophy as you want. Can be taller than you, if that will make you happy."

Hell. He'd buy her a trophy as big as a house to keep that smile on her face.

"Oh, I have no need for a trophy, but thank you for the offer," she said in a sweet-as-sugar sort of way. He liked that, too. "I think the winner should be able to choose their prize. But it has to involve the loser. So, if you win, your prize involves me doing something for you or with you. Whatever you want, within reason. And I get the same choice if I win."

Hmm. Well, then. He wasn't so sure what would be better, being on the winning or losing end of that deal. It would prove interesting to see what she'd choose as her "prize" if she won and, okay, if he won? He might just ask her about the details of that dream, so long as he could figure out a way to do so without sounding as corny as a lovestruck teenager.

"You have a deal," he said, scratching his jaw. "I've been thinking for a while now of having the house painted. Think you could handle that? I'd buy all the supplies, of course, and even some how-to books if you were to need them. Might go that direction, supposing I win."

She scrunched her nose. "I would say that painting your house does not fall in the 'within reason' category, so nope, you'll have to come up with something else. Supposing you win."

"Okay, sure, I can come up with something else." He grinned, enjoying this exchange more than any of their other conversations thus far. "Only question that remains is…what game should be the tie breaker? One we've already played or something different?"

"Something different, of course." Walking to the pile of games he'd brought out earlier, she looked through them, one by one. "Lots of choices here. Do you have a preference?"

He narrowed his eyes, took stock of the various games—some meant for families, some for adults and some bought with his niece in mind—and considered a few of the strategy games. He excelled in those. But really, he was far more curious to see what Goldi would choose, so in the end, he shook his head. "Nope. No preference. You pick, I'll play."

She laughed, instantly reaching for a game, and damn it, why did the glow from the fireplace have to send a shimmer of light through her hair, making it resemble spun gold? Or what he assumed spun gold would look like. And what was wrong with him to notice such a thing, anyway? It took every ounce of willpower to stay seated, to not walk over and…well, hell, touch her hair. Like a kid reaching for a piece of chocolate he should *not* have.

Swallowing hard, he forced his attention from the shimmering spectacle of her hair to the box in her hands, and all comparisons to spun gold evaporated.

"Really?" he said. Hell. He'd never even played that game. He'd bought it last year as a gift for Cassie's birthday, but she already had it. He'd brought it back home for when she visited, but they'd yet to actually play. "All those choices and you think that should be the game that decides the championship?"

Returning to the couch, she set the game on the coffee table. "I picked it, didn't I? But I have an excellent reason why. Neither of us have ever played this game, so we're starting at ground zero. No one has an advantage. That seems appropriate for a tie breaker."

"Excellent point, but how do you know I haven't played it before?"

She reached over and picked at the plastic still coating the box. "Original packaging, never been opened," she said, grinning. "And I seriously doubt you've sat around with your, um—photographer buddies?—with beer and munchies over a game of Hedbanz."

"More excellent points," he admitted. "And you're right on every one of them."

Except for the photographer buddy thing. Oh, he had a few close friends, but they didn't exactly hang out over beer or munchies playing anything. Only reason he had all these games was for Fiona and Cassie. They tended to get bored real fast when visiting. Didn't stop them from showing up at least once a week when he was around. His sister insisted on family togetherness, on being *present*.

He knew why. Their parents had died when they were young, and she'd gone to live with their aunt while he'd lived with his grandfather. They'd missed a lot of years together, and Fiona had never really gotten over that, never stopped longing for what they hadn't had.

Well, that and her stubbornness. The woman never gave in on a damn thing, even when doing so would be easier. "Why don't you read the rules while I grab us some of those munchies you mentioned?" he asked. "You can fill me in when I get back."

"Sure thing," she said, already picking open the plastic covering. Lifting her eyes to his, she smiled. "Bring lots of sustenance. You'll need it to survive the loss."

"Is that so?"

"That is so."

"We'll see about that," he said, heading toward the kitchen and keeping his smile to himself.

Tough talk. With the way she'd invaded his brain, she

probably would win. And that was fine. Surely, she'd smile again then, which should further lessen the awkwardness between them from earlier.

She'd made him lunch. She hadn't wanted to disturb him, but she'd thought about his welfare. It made the memory of that morning's Swedish pop group alarm, and his grumpiness about it, extinguish as if it had never occurred. Funny. Thoughtful. Caring. Sweet. All words that described this…stranger. Beautiful, too, without doubt.

Strikingly so, even without makeup and clothes that properly fit.

Liam put together a plate of cheese, crackers and grapes and poured them each a fresh cup of coffee.

Before returning to the living room, he went through the back door and stepped outside. The storm had calmed considerably. The wind still blew strong, but there wasn't nearly as much snow falling.

Yup. The storm was gearing down. Very likely by tomorrow afternoon, the roads would start to get cleared and within another twenty-four hours he'd be able to cart Miss Goldilocks to her friend's house. He'd have his space again. His quiet.

And that would be that.

Chapter Seven

Hedbanz, as it turned out, was insanely easy. Guess "what" or "who" you were by asking questions to the other players—in this case, Liam—for a yes or no response. The "who" or "what" was displayed on a card bound to your forehead with a headband. You couldn't see it, but those you were playing with could.

Meredith won, but only by a single point and only due to the fact that after several rounds of being an animal—how unfair was that, seeing that he earned his living by photographing wildlife?—Liam had the misfortune of choosing the "I am a flashlight" card. He was stuck with being a flashlight for several rounds, his questions not getting him close enough for a correct guess, which allowed her ample opportunity to move ahead and win.

Which she did, with the "I am bacon" card. She'd narrowed it down to being a food, asked if it was mostly eaten at breakfast, if it fell into the meat category and finally, if she'd made it that morning. With a sigh and a quick roll of his eyes, she had the answer. She'd never loved bacon quite so much as she did at that moment, because now...*now*...she'd earned the right to request something from Liam without feeling guilty.

She hadn't yet decided what that something should be, but she'd figure that out soon. She'd have to. It looked as if tomorrow would be the last full day she'd be here alone with Liam. Unless fortune truly shone on her shoulders and another storm swept in while they slept. Unlikely, but hey, that she was even here at all was even more so.

"Sure you wouldn't prefer a trophy?" Liam asked as they picked up the game and put the various pieces back in the box. "Or...a Harry & David gift basket? Fruit-of-the-month club?" He winked and her heart dropped to her stomach. Over a wink. That had never happened to her before, with anyone. Even Rico. "I know! A year's supply of bacon. That seems fitting."

"None of those ideas include you," she said. "Remember the deal?"

"They do include me, since I would be the one supplying you with a trophy, gift basket, a fruit-of-the-month subscription or a year's supply of bacon." Another wink, followed by a semisarcastic grin. "Not sure how you can state otherwise!"

"They do not include you in the way I would like," she said, surprised by her forthrightness. But hey, it was time to start living, right? "And before you ask, no, I don't know what exactly I'm going to ask for my prize yet. But when I know I will let you in on it."

Leaning over the coffee table so they were mere inches apart, he said, "And will your prize fall within the reasonable range? I mean, you're not going to ask me to drive you to New York or take you on a vacation to Hawaii or anything of that nature, are you?"

"Um…no. Nothing like that." Lord, he smelled good. It wasn't the scent of a cologne or aftershave or even his soap or shampoo. He didn't smell like trees or the air after a drenching rain or anything so defined. It was just him. And it was good. Welcoming and appealing and sexy all rolled into one package.

She drew in a breath, a rather large one, and worked to modulate her voice, saying, "And of course it will be reasonable. Probably fun, too. I just have to think some on the actual specifics of what that will entail."

A whisper of a wish slipped into being. A kiss. She could ask for a kiss. That would be fun. Reasonable, however? Not so much.

Besides which, if this man ever kissed her, it needed to be of his own free will. Because he just *had* to. Because the thought of not kissing her would be unbearable. Unthinkable.

Heat rushed her cheeks, soaked into her skin and swept through her limbs until her fingers and toes tingled. Great. Now all she could think of was kissing this man, of what his mouth would feel like on hers, of how her body would respond to his touch. And he was so close. If she pushed herself forward a few more inches, if she were courageous enough, she could kiss him before he even realized what was happening.

Quickly, before the wish fueled a type of courage she didn't really want to have—at least not yet—she stood and picked up the game. "I suppose we should put everything away and…and…" What? It was too soon for sleep, they'd eaten enough snacks to not need dinner, there wasn't a television that she'd seen and even if there was, she doubted they'd have reception. Even a generator couldn't fix that. "I guess I don't know what we should do then."

"Now you sound like my niece," Liam said, also standing. "We could play a few more games, or...well, would you be interested in seeing some of my photographs?" He blinked as he asked the question, as if he'd surprised himself. "Or...let's just go with another game."

"Oh, no you don't. Once an offer like that is made, there is no taking it back!" Before he could argue further, she stacked several of the games in her arms. "These go in the mudroom?"

"Yeah. I can put them away. I need to let out the dogs anyway."

"And I can help."

"Stubborn," he said, half under his breath. "And really, I don't expect you to want to look at photographs. I'm not sure why I suggested it, but—"

"Liam," she said, interrupting him, her voice soft. "I already asked you questions about your work this morning, remember? I am very interested in seeing what you do, and I am honored you're willing to show me. Please don't take that away. Okay?"

His gaze dropped to the floor, which surprised her, but he nodded. "Okay. On both accounts, but as soon as you want to do something else, just say the word."

"Oh, I doubt that will happen. But yeah, you have a deal." Surely, he was accustomed to people viewing his photographs if this was his profession. Yet, he seemed shy at the idea, even though he was the one who'd broached it. Another interesting facet of this man she'd dreamed about. Another tidbit of information to store with the rest.

So far, she very much liked what she knew.

"Well, then," he said, that gruff tone returning to his voice. "I guess I can't argue."

"No, you really can't."

They put away the games, he let out Max and Maggie and less than twenty minutes later, he was opening the door to his office.

And she felt privileged, somehow, to be let into the wizard's inner sanctum. A place, she was sure, not many people had entered. She didn't take this lightly. She knew, in the way a person really knows something, that Liam didn't easily share his privacy.

The room was larger than she'd imagined, rectangle in shape. Windows that almost went from floor to ceiling occupied the wall directly across from the door. Against this wall of windows was his desk—long and sturdy—upon which sat three oversize monitors, boxes in various shapes and sizes that she assumed held...well, photography odds and ends, a couple of framed photos that must be of his sister and niece and an impressive stack of notebooks, sketch pads and file folders.

The back wall seemed to be formed from shelves from the ground up and storage containers, so many that she couldn't even see the wall behind them, along with camera cases and other paraphernalia of one sort or another. The bottommost shelf held several oversize duffel bags that appeared to be full. What he stored in those, she couldn't say.

There was also a large refrigerator to her right and next to that, another door. A second bathroom, maybe? Or a darkroom. The latter of those two possibilities made the most sense.

While there were a lot of items in this room, everything appeared neat and orderly—save for the tottering stack of files, notebooks and sketchbooks on his desk—

which didn't surprise her. She'd already noticed Liam's preference for tidiness. Oh, he didn't seem obsessive about it, but to her, he was obviously a man who believed that everything had its place.

Meredith believed in the same, but she also didn't mind a little clutter every now and again. Her grandmother used to say that the messy bits were where real life happened. Meredith tended to agree with that assessment, more so today than ever before.

Clearing his throat, Liam gently took hold of her arm and guided her to the center of the room. He turned her toward the long wall across from his desk and said, "There. Some of my photographs. My personal favorites, I guess you could say."

And oh. Just...oh.

She blinked at the display, let out a breath and blinked again. If someone had blindfolded her and led her to this precise spot with this precise view, she would've stated with unequivocal certainty that she was standing in an art gallery and that these photographs were taken by someone at the top of his or her career.

There were large photographs, small ones and those that fell in a myriad of sizes in between. And all were... well, she didn't have a word that could capture every one.

Some were beautiful. Some were striking. Some, to her, were melancholy...almost sad. There were those that evoked the sensation of joy and togetherness and those that resonated of loneliness. There were close-ups and distance shots, those captured in a hazy, dreamlike manner and those that were so crisp and clear, she could have been there in the moment, rather than simply looking at a photograph of one.

All of them, though, were breathtaking and rich with emotion.

She saw pride and focus in the loyal stance of a muscled lion, giggling, playful mirth in the gazes of chubby, tumbling wolf pups and fierce love in the mama wolf standing sentry. In another, three multicolored birds—she didn't know their type—were perched on a long, curvy branch, their eyes curious and intent on the camera, and she knew they were but a millisecond from taking off in flight. She saw a pile of sleepy monkeys, so entwined with each other that it was difficult to see which limbs belonged to which monkey, a herd of elephants studiously guiding their young and a rather large lizard that might have been a Komodo dragon surrounded by green foliage, staring upward at a vibrant purple butterfly.

While she looked, while she thought and felt, Liam stood silently next to her, waiting, without expression, his body tense.

Still uncomfortable? Why? Obviously, this man wasn't merely a talented photographer, he was successful. His home and the equipment in this room told her that much. Success in a creative career typically meant that others viewed your work on a consistent basis. Surely, he'd had plenty of experience in this by now?

Though, perhaps he wasn't used to standing in the same room while someone looked over his work. Especially in this room, in his house where he lived with his two dogs and no one else on the side of a mountain. A private man. A quiet man. So, okay, his discomfort made sense.

The sudden want to comfort, to be there for him, had Meredith reaching for Liam's hand. He jerked slightly as she wove her fingers through his, but he didn't pull away.

"Thank you," she said. "So very much."

"For what?"

"Letting me in here. Showing me what you do. I know this isn't easy for you."

"You're welcome." He cleared his throat a second time. "Truth is, I wanted to or I wouldn't have offered and…it's easier than I thought it would be."

"Good." And then, "Your pictures are in magazines, aren't they?"

"Yes."

"Has one ever been on the cover of *National Geographic*?"

"Yes."

"Have several made it to the cover?"

"Yes," he said.

"How many?" The minute she could, she would be scouring her local library's magazine collection, hoping to find those covers. He didn't answer, so she repeated, "How many?"

"Enough of them."

"That isn't an appropriate answer! But okay, where else are your photographs?"

"Framed prints. Posters. Calendars. A few books." Tugging on her hand, he started to lead her out of the room, but she planted her heels and stayed put. "Come on, Miss Nosy. If you're done with the questions, we should—"

"Oh, I'm far from done," she said, interrupting him before he could suggest they return to more board games. "I've barely had a chance to really look. And I don't know the stories."

He inhaled a breath, gave her hand a gentle squeeze. "The goal is for the audience to create their own story, from what they see. From what they feel. That job is yours, my dear."

"I already have, but…I want to know yours." She

turned, faced Liam and forced herself to meet his eyes with hers. Never easy. Not when his eyes beckoned and pulled her in, made her want more than she should. "Will you tell me your story behind them? Where you were, what you were you feeling? Why these particular shots and why they made it to this wall when I'm sure you have thousands of other photographs that are equally beautiful? Please?"

Dark, ridiculously long lashes fluttered as he blinked. If only she could have those lashes, she'd never have a need for mascara again.

He let go of her hand and shook his head, his mouth already forming the word *no*. She was ready for this, had another slew of arguments all set to go because she did not want to leave this room without hearing Liam's voice adding depth to his work. It felt necessary, somehow. As necessary as food and water and air.

But then he surprised her again. He closed his mouth, shook his head a second time and said, "If this is what you want, then okay, I will tell you…my stories."

"It is what I want." Oh. Did he think this was her prize for winning Hedbanz? If it had to be to get him to talk, she'd absolutely go that route, but she kept that information to herself. "And thank you for your willingness to share. I'm guessing it isn't something you're used to?"

"It's happened before, but no… I tend to keep to myself."

"Shocker," she said lightly. "That seems so out of character."

A brow lifted and his lips split into a grin. "Any more sarcasm and I'll take back my offer and you'll never know any of my stories, Miss Goldilocks." Another long-lashed blink. "Ah… Meredith. Sorry about that, but in my head, you're Goldi."

"I don't mind." Until this moment, she hadn't realized that Goldi was a nickname for Goldilocks. She wasn't sure if that was a compliment or something less. "I am curious, however. Why Goldilocks?"

"Really? You have to ask?" Tugging on a strand of her long, blond hair, he said, "Well, there's the hair and the fact that you invaded my home and passed out on my couch."

"But I did not eat your porridge or break anything!"

"Well, you haven't broken anything yet," he said. "Though, you did manage to make quite a mess earlier. I'd say that's close enough."

"We already agreed that wasn't my fault," she said with a toss of her head. "And I had no real choice but to invade your home, but you and your two dogs could absolutely be the three bears…and wasn't the papa bear really, really grumpy?"

"Grumpy? Nah. He was just misunderstood."

She laughed. "Is that what they're calling it nowadays?"

"Yes, Miss Sass, it is."

"Well, in my book, that isn't—" The room spun as a sudden wave of dizziness overtook her, forcing her to blindly reach out for something to grab onto.

Liam's arms came around her and he pulled her close to keep her standing. And he didn't let go.

"Now, see," he said, his voice soft, "this is what I was worried about. You should've rested today. I should have insisted you rest. But instead—"

"I'm fine, and I did rest. I sat on my butt and played games most of the afternoon and evening. You were with me, so you should know I didn't do anything strenuous." But okay, in this second, she felt as if she'd run a marathon at full throttle without eating for days. Not that she would tell Liam that. He'd drag her to the sofa and she wouldn't hear any of his stories.

Worse, this lovely moment would end. She didn't want that.

"You're not fine. You're pale and trembling." A long sigh emerged. "Come on, let me help you to the living room. We'll get you settled and—"

"Oh, no you don't, mister," she said with every ounce of strength she could muster. "You were about to tell me about your photographs. You're not getting off that easy."

Another sigh, longer and deeper than the one before. "Don't ask me to ignore your well-being in favor of more talking. Because it isn't going to happen."

He started to tug her toward the door, so she did the only thing she could by pulling herself loose and dropping to the floor. Before he could think that she'd fainted or something and pick her up and carry her away, she tossed him a satisfied grin. "See what I did here? Now I can rest and listen to your stories at the same time. We both get what we want."

A third sigh emerged. "Sitting on the floor is not the same as lying down. You know this as well as I do." She didn't respond, just continued to smile up at him while he stared at her with...incredulity? Humor? She wasn't sure, but she didn't see annoyance. "Fine," he said after a short pause. "You win. Kind of, but you're not sitting on the floor."

He pulled his chair out from his desk and rolled it her way. Well, that was fine. She wouldn't argue about sitting in a chair over the floor. "Thank you, Liam," she said, carefully standing. "I think this works quite well as a compromise."

"Compromise, hmm?" he said. "We can call it that if you wish."

She sat down and waited a second for her head to stop spinning before asking, "What else would you call it?"

"That I recognize mule-headed stubbornness when I see it and that I would have to bodily carry you to the couch to get my way." He ran his hand over his jaw. "And don't think I didn't consider that idea, because I did. I'm just fairly sure you'd stomp back in here, and we'd be right where we started. Figured I'd save us a few steps."

"Right. A compromise."

Between them, the air simmered with unsaid words. Again, she asked herself how this man could feel so familiar to her. Solely because of her dream? Maybe. Or maybe she'd had the dream due to this sense of *knowing*. What came first, the chicken or the egg?

A laugh almost broke free, but she held it in. "You should get a chair, too," she said. "So you can sit next to me."

"I'm good," he said. "Let's just…"

"Get this over with?"

"Something like that." Walking forward, he pointed to the photograph of the three multicolored birds, inhaled a breath and, a second later, shook his head. "There isn't really anything to tell with this one," he said after a rather long pause. "Just three pretty birds."

Shadows existed there in his voice, and a bolt of tension ripped through his body. Meredith's senses went on alert, and she wondered—worried a little, too—about the reason for whatever darkness existed and how a photograph of three birds could be the cause. Should she say anything? Stay quiet? In the end, she went with her instincts and said, "Oh, I doubt that. I mean, they're on your wall of fame, right? There has to be a reason?"

Another inhale and he turned just enough away that she could no longer see his face. But then, he nodded and started talking. "The paradise tanager is an outgoing, social breed of bird found in the Amazon Basin. They're songbirds, restless and active, and don't tend to stay in any one place for very long. They group together, typically in clusters of five or more. Like a…um…family, I suppose you could say. Traveling together, protecting each other."

He went on to describe how they foraged for food, their nesting habits, along with a variety of other information one could find on the internet or in a book. The darkness was no longer evident, and in fact he spoke easily, with knowledge, but now his tone reminded Meredith of a school teacher giving a lesson.

She listened quietly, mostly watching his body language and wishing she could see his eyes. Even if only for a heartbeat.

What he didn't talk about—what she guessed he was purposely leaving out—were the personal details she'd asked for. What was in his head when he took this photograph, how did he feel, what was going on for him in that moment and why had this particular photograph made it to this wall?

Even so, she remained silent and listened, hoping something—anything—personal would creep into his verbiage. She yearned to know more about this man, from the smallest detail to the largest. She ached to know what had caused his change in demeanor.

But she couldn't ask those questions. They were too private, given the darkness she'd heard, which meant that he likely wouldn't answer them anyway.

One by one, Liam went through the photographs in the same manner as he had with the paradise tanager shot, his voice calm and smooth, knowledgeable and yeah… impersonal. Not quite flat, but without offering anything to connect the man behind the camera with these incredible works of art.

Whatever memories those "three pretty birds" evoked seemed to have stuck around for the duration. She hated that, but despite how much she wished he'd open up a little and despite the questions circling in her brain, she still didn't interrupt.

There wasn't any reason to. She had the sense that no matter what she might say in this moment, her questions wouldn't achieve the desired result. He'd have to get there on his own, due to a want to share with *her*. That was something you couldn't push a person into doing. All she could do was listen to what he chose to share. Even if that amounted to nothing more than a bunch of basic facts.

So, she listened. And she wondered. And she worried. Tomorrow was possibly her last full day to spend here, in this house that was hidden in the mountains, with a man like no one she'd ever known before. What if, when she left here, she never saw Liam again?

The thought sobered her further and weighed heavier than it should. Quickly, before the heaviness could take root, she shoved practical, reasonable thoughts into her head. Life would go on. She'd visit with Rachel and figure out where to go from here.

Her original plan still existed. Nothing had changed. And the honest truth of the matter was that nothing *should* change. There was a lot of rocky, uneven ground to cover before she would be ready to truly consider the wishes and wants that now swam in her heart.

Right. Because how could she have the life she'd dreamed about—whether with Liam or another man she'd yet to meet—before she realized some of her own goals? How could she really know someone else or let anyone fully into her world before she really knew herself and what she was made of?

So, okay. Nothing had changed. Her focus remained the same, on her future and creating a life of her own making. That goal needed to come to fruition, and none of what she felt—or thought she felt—toward Liam held any bearing.

But that didn't mean she could erase her concern or her curiosity, and that didn't mean that she wouldn't enjoy the rest of her time here with him. And there was no chance that she would walk away and forget.

Because she wouldn't. Couldn't.

If her dream held any true importance, if fate had brought her here for a reason, she would eventually know that as surely as she knew her own name. She wouldn't have to question or guess or push or prod. All she had to do was follow her path and see where it led. See if Liam's path merged with hers again at some point in the future. She hoped it would.

She returned her attention to him, to the steady, calm beat of his voice as he spoke about the wolf cubs and the mama standing sentry. His body was still angled away from hers, but she would guess he wore a serious expression and a hooded gaze. The unnamed darkness still had its hold, and she felt for him. Wanted and wished for lightness to enter his speech, for a rolling laugh to emerge, for a ray of sunlight to overtake that darkness and send it scurrying for cover.

All at once, an idea of what she would ask for as her "prize" blossomed into being.

Maybe she only had one more day with this man. Maybe she couldn't offer the light he seemed to need at this moment, but she could use her prize to elicit some frivolity. And he'd have to say yes, because her request absolutely fell into the reasonable range.

They would have fun. There would hopefully be laughter. And perhaps that would be a gift to Liam, as well as to herself. If nothing else, they would create another memory she would carry with her, along with the rest, as she forged a future she could call her own.

Leaving Liam and his sanctuary didn't have to be sad. Not if she could help it.

Chapter Eight

For the second day in a row, Liam woke up grumpy. Today, though, he couldn't place blame on a Swedish pop group or Meredith's choice to play "Mamma Mia" at a louder than decent volume. The house was whisper silent when he opened his eyes, still more dark than light outside and as had already become the norm, his dogs were nowhere to be seen.

They were, without a doubt, curled up with Goldilocks. And even the absence of his traitorous dogs didn't account for his sour mood. If anything, he figured Max and Maggie had the better end of the sleeping deal. How could he fault them for that?

Punching his pillow, Liam rolled over and closed his eyes. He tried to force his body to relax and his brain to stop its incessant thinking in the hope that maybe, just maybe, he could catch a tad more sleep.

He hadn't slept well. Every hour or so, he'd wake and

thoughts of the woman downstairs would be merged with Christy, with that god-awful loss, and he'd toss and turn for another thirty minutes before drifting off again. He hated that.

It had taken so long to come to terms with losing his wife and child. So damn long he'd worked to make peace with what couldn't be changed. And now, a few days with Meredith and all that muck had churned to the surface.

That accounted for his bad mood. He never wanted to return to those days of barely being able to breathe without feeling that sharp, incapacitating pain.

Very purposefully, Liam turned his thoughts away from Christy, away from Meredith and instead focused on the day ahead. The activities that required his attention.

He couldn't really do a lot more workwise until power was restored. The generator kept the house livable, but the PCs were a major power drain and he wouldn't risk developing prints. Yesterday, when he'd sequestered himself in his office, he'd spent the majority of his time organizing the digital photographs on his laptop until the battery had gotten too low to continue. And then, he'd spent another solid hour dozing in his chair. That was why he hadn't heard Meredith's knock, why he hadn't known she'd left him a meal outside his door.

And that was all it took for his mind to once again focus on what he did *not* want to focus on. Which also meant that any additional sleep was out of the question. He was up for the duration, which meant he might as well—

Music.

ABBA again interrupted his thoughts, and he felt his mouth stretch into a smile. A wide enough one that his cheeks hurt from the effort. And the fact that the smile came on its own accord, so quickly and so naturally, didn't escape his analytical brain.

This woman was something special. Someone special.

And that made her even more dangerous. To his peace of mind, to the lifestyle that had saved him from being buried alive, to holding on to his sanity and every other damn thing he'd worked so hard to achieve since losing Christy, their baby and the future he'd believed was theirs for the taking. The future that would've existed, if not for the winds of fate. An unstoppable force, one you couldn't predict or, in any true fashion, protect yourself from.

But that very same force had brought Goldi to his couch.

Standing, Liam strode to his bedroom window and pulled back the curtain. The snow had stopped. Not so much as a flurry whisked through the early morning air. It would take a full day, he knew from prior experience, before he'd have any possibility of safely escorting Meredith into Steamboat Springs. So, fate had brought her to him, and now with the end of the storm, fate was allowing—encouraging?—her departure? Possibly.

And maybe, just maybe, a twinge of regret lived alongside his relief.

"Of the many, many possibilities you could ask for as a prize, this is what you're going with?" Liam asked Meredith later that day.

His expression was a solid mix of shock and good humor. The good humor appealed obviously, but Meredith kind of enjoyed surprising him, too. She had the feeling he wasn't used to being surprised.

"Didn't you spend enough time outside in the snow the other night? One would think that experience would be enough to last a lifetime."

Ha. If he thought that would change her mind, he was very much wrong. "That was different, which you know full well." She avoided looking him straight in the eye. Every time she did that, she fell a little more. A little harder. "I won fair and square."

They were dressed similarly, in jeans and sweatshirts. Her clothes hadn't yet been washed, but they were dry and serviceable enough for a couple of hours outside. And okay, she maybe felt a little bad at making him spend more time outside—he'd been out there most of the morning, clearing snow from the porch and pathways— but not bad enough to give in on her prize.

They were going to build a snowman together. And darn it all, one way or another, she planned on eliciting at least one laugh from him before they were done. Somehow.

"That's a point." He gave her one of those long, searching looks before asking, "You're sure you're up for it? You weren't doing all that well last night."

"I'm feeling great. So we're agreed?"

"Sure, if this is really what you want." He gave his head a quick shake. "But I don't know, if I were you, I'd definitely be going for the Harry & David fruit-of-the-month club."

"Good thing you're not me, then! But…um, I will need some gloves. And maybe a hat and a scarf? If you have any extras I could borrow." And then, before he could use that as an excuse to weasel out of her plan, she continued with, "If you don't, I'll just use socks again."

"Uh-huh, as if I'd allow such a thing." He went upstairs and returned a scant minute later with a pair of gloves. "There are a few extra hats and scarves in the mudroom. What else do we need? I have never actually constructed a person made of snow before."

Meredith had been in the process of putting on her coat, but Liam's words stopped her midzip. "Are you joking?" she asked. "Because I have never met a person over the age of four who hasn't built a snowman."

"I spent most of my childhood years in Florida, with my grandfather."

She waited for him to say more, but he didn't. There were so many obvious questions, but how could she ask them? Why he grew up "mostly" with his grandfather wasn't her business.

"I was hoping you'd give me an answer I could use as fodder for picking on you," she said in a teasing sort of way. "But no, you had to go with a perfectly logical response."

Shrugging, he tossed her the gloves, which she—surprisingly—managed to catch. "Just the facts, ma'am, just the facts. So are we ready?"

"Well, we need a carrot and...you wouldn't happen to have a bag of coal lying around, would you? Maybe a handful of buttons?" She finished zipping her coat and slid on the gloves. They were meant for Liam's hands, so they were loose, but she didn't mind. "Oh, another scarf!"

"You take this snowman stuff pretty seriously, huh? I don't know what I have lying around, but I'll see what I can come up with."

Did she hear a hint of frustration? Maybe. "Or, you know, it doesn't really matter," she said. "We can use sticks and stones and whatever else we can find. The goal is to have fun."

"Right. Fun," he said over his shoulder as he headed toward the kitchen. "Let's go do this, before it gets any colder out there."

Yup. Definitely frustration. Due to her and her choice of a prize—which was supposed to be silly and lighthearted—or due to the admission that he'd been raised by his grandfather and the unspoken story behind the statement? Or something else entirely?

This, like so many other aspects of Liam's personality, she couldn't hazard a guess. The man just did not give enough away for any shot at an accurate prediction. She thought he was that way with everybody, so the short time they had known each other didn't really come into play.

Her goal hadn't changed, though. One laugh, that was all she needed to coax from him. Come hell or high water, another freak snowstorm, or some other out-of-the-ordinary event, she would get that laugh. It seemed of the utmost importance, even if she didn't know why.

"Goldi?" Liam's voice, the volume of which was just shy of a bona fide shout, hit her ears. "Do you want to build this damn snowman or not?"

"You bet I do," she said under her breath. *One* laugh. How hard could that be? Following the same path he'd taken less than a minute ago, she called out, "On my way!"

She found him standing in the mudroom, holding a long, purple scarf and a matching knit hat. His sister's or an old girlfriend's? Or hell, maybe he had a current girlfriend. Who knew, and yup, that was yet another series of questions she refused to ask, albeit for different reasons than all the others she'd smothered so far.

Accepting the scarf and hat, she quickly put them on and then, offering him a grin, said, "Well, what are we waiting for? I'm ready. Are you?"

"Sure. Ready enough anyway," he said in a sandpaper-dry voice. He whistled and Max and Maggie ran to the door, tails wagging. Well, at least they were excited.

"You're in charge of this expedition, by the way. Tell me what you want me to do and I'll do it."

Finally, because she had to say *something* even if it wasn't what she really wanted to say, she said, "Are you okay? I mean, if you really don't want to do this, that's fine."

Those ridiculously beautiful eyes of his found hers, and there it was again…that spark of attraction that sizzled and popped in her blood.

"I'm fine," he said. "Just feeling antsy today, ready for everything to get back to normal. But I suppose every man should build a snowman once in his lifetime, and I likely never would have without prodding."

Not an enthusiastic response, but she'd take it. Happily, even.

He held the door open, allowing Max and Maggie to take off in an exuberant run. Meredith went next, stepping carefully onto the recently cleared path, and waited for Liam.

The snow was piled in uneven slopes brought on by the high winds, and the trees were weighted and almost completely white. It was beautiful and quiet and deeply spiritual in its serenity. She had the out-there realization that she could live here, in this silent sanctuary, without any trouble whatsoever.

She might even be happier here than she'd ever been before in her life.

A nice thought, but not exactly a feasible one. Forcing a smile, she turned toward Liam. "I think we should make our snowman over there," she said, pointing toward a relatively flat section of snow in front of a cluster of fir trees and a single towering aspen. "He'll look good over there and easily visible from the house. What do you think?"

"Ah... I'm not sure that's a good idea, Meredith. Consider—"

"It's a great idea, Mr. Grump," she interrupted. If this continued, she might have to smack him with a snowball or two. "My prize, right? I should get to choose."

A brow raised, but he nodded. "Mr. Grump, is it?" Shielding his gaze with one hand, he looked toward the area she'd already pointed out. "Perhaps I am simply confused and incorrectly identifying the spot you're after. Why don't you walk over there and show me where you mean? I'm quite sure that will help me visualize what you've so easily seen."

"I can do that." Pleased he'd shown any interest, she walked off the shoveled path toward the section of trees she'd chosen. Initially, she didn't have too much trouble, as the snow directly around the path wasn't that high, probably because Liam had leveled it out some. But as she continued her forward motion, that quickly changed.

She stopped and looked down, saw the snow had already reached about midcalf and she wasn't even at the deepest portion yet. Reconsidering, she turned around, only to see Liam watching her with his arms crossed over his chest and wearing a smart-ass grin. The brat! He'd known and hadn't said a thing.

Well. He'd tried to. She'd interrupted him, sure he was hip-deep in grump mode. Of course, she should've considered the snow obstacle on her own.

"Problem?" Liam asked, his smile widening another notch. "That can't be the spot you meant, is it? I really misunderstood, then. I thought you wanted it nearer the trees?"

"Well, I did."

"But?"

"It seems as if I—"

"Yes? Do tell. Is there a problem? Something you want to share?" His lips twitched in an almost laugh. "Having second thoughts, are you?"

"Nope. No problem. No second thoughts." Narrowing her eyes, she shrugged. "I…ah… I just wanted to be sure you were paying attention and not playing with the dogs."

"Never fear, Goldi. At this moment, you have my undivided attention."

Yeah. She bet she did. "Good!" And with that, she turned around again, dead-set on getting herself through the snow and to those trees.

To prove what, exactly? And why? She didn't have an answer for either question other than pure stubbornness. In her book, that was more than enough reason. Even if the stance fell on the slightly childish side.

She pushed through another few feet, the level of the snow creeping upward as she slogged forward. Another few feet and she just about had to climb out of the snow for each step as it had almost reached her knees. No amount of sheer stubbornness would get her the rest of the way without tumbling face-first into the snow. And if that happened, she had zero doubt that Liam would insist she go inside and change into another pair of his pajamas and rest.

So maybe this hadn't been a true battle of wills, but she sort of felt as if he had won. Which was fine, she supposed. Maybe that would put him in a better mood for the rest of the day. Giving up, she faced Liam and shrugged. "Can't get there," she said. "Snow is too high."

"Reason over stubbornness, eh? I wondered how far you'd take it."

"Just enjoying the view, huh?"

"Something like that, but another step or two and I

would've stopped you. I don't want you to fall again," he said. "Be careful coming back, okay?"

His words soothed. Warmed her heart, too. "I'll be fine. Just have to follow the same—" And naturally, because she was focused on talking and not her movement, she didn't lift her right leg high enough to clear the ledge she'd created on her way in, and yup, she fell. Face-first.

The heavy snow surrounded her body, almost sucking her in as she imagined quicksand would, burying her face and leaving her without the ability to breathe. A now familiar terror, one she'd sincerely hoped she'd never experience again, erupted into being. Really? She'd survived being lost in the middle of a snowstorm, but she couldn't pick herself up out of this?

Pressing her arms downward, she pushed with all her might, and just as she did, Liam's arms came around her and pulled her up. To him. To safety and oxygen and a pair of green eyes filled with fear that mirrored her own. Suddenly, the very last thing she cared about was building a damn snowman.

"You okay?" Liam asked, his hold on her secure, his gaze glued to hers.

She could barely breathe, let alone talk, but she managed an "I am now, yes."

"Okay. Good." He picked her up as if she weighed little more than a can of beans and carried her in the direction of the house. "I'm sorry, Goldi. I shouldn't have let you walk out here, but I really didn't think you'd go so far. Of course, if you had let me talk to begin with," he said with teasing candor, "we'd be halfway done with that snowman by now."

He smelled good. He felt good. She still couldn't breathe correctly, but that had zip to do with her tumble in the snow. It had everything to do with the man holding her. "You're right. But you were so grouchy! So, really, the fault is on both of our shoulders."

"Hmm. I wonder if there is ever a time you're not stubborn?"

"Hmm," she mimicked, "I wonder the same about you."

He kept carrying her as he treaded through the thick snow. The fact he could with so little effort astounded her. Made her feel…feminine and fragile and as if his primary goal was to protect her, which okay, at this moment that was the case. And strangely, as much as she'd pushed against her father's various ways of protecting her, in this scenario with Liam, she found she didn't mind at all. He…well, he made her feel safe, rather than little more than a porcelain doll.

"You…ah…can probably put me down now. I'm guessing I can walk the rest of the way without falling."

"I'll put you down when we're inside and not a second before." He let out a sigh. "Sorry, but you're going to have to cross that snowman off your list, because it's not happening."

Oh. The snowman. She'd already forgotten, because now, there was only one thought in her head. Just one. And it had nothing to do with making Liam laugh.

She wanted a kiss. Yearned for a kiss. The possibility bopped around in her head a bit, and unlike last night, she determined it was a reasonable request. They were both consenting adults. She'd won fair and square and had earned herself a prize. He might object, but she could certainly ask.

And now, the thought of not kissing Liam, of not knowing what his lips felt like on hers seemed…impossible. She had to know.

Would he reject her request? She had the belief that

he wouldn't. Or that he wouldn't, at the very least, out-right refuse the proposition. "I'm in total agreement," she said. "We can nix the snowman in lieu of another prize."

"Giving up that easily? Did you conk your head on a rock when you fell?"

"I did not! But there is something else, something... better, that I'd like for my prize. Now that you've ve-toed my snowman." It was one thing to decide the ask-ing made sense; it was another to actually verbalize the question. "I'm pretty sure it will make me far happier than the snowman would've. No. Not pretty sure. Ab-solutely sure."

She could still back out if she lost her courage. She hadn't given anything away yet.

"That was quick." He paused at the door, looked down at her and said, "Let me guess. More talking? I suppose— under great duress, mind you—I can agree to that."

If a kiss hadn't become her goal, she might've agreed. Mostly due to Liam's pained expression at the possibility of exposing more of himself via a conversation. It was vulnerable and disarming, and the fact that he was will-ing to go there if that was what she wanted showed her a lot about the man behind that expression. Maybe more than she'd seen before.

"No worries. I'm not going to ask you to talk."

Relief etched his face, easing the lines around his mouth. "Really? Gotta say, Goldi, that's surprising. You've barely stopped talking since you've been here."

"Right. Because a near-comatose woman has so much to say," she fired back.

"All right, you have a point. I will amend my state-ment to reflect that you've barely stopped talking since we officially met." He winked and her heart spun. It was that simple. That powerful. "How's that? Better?"

"Much. But no, what I'm thinking of requires very little talking. If any at all. In fact, no talking would probably be best, because, well…"

Lovely. Now she was rambling. But how could she not while this man held her smelling like he did? Looking at her as he did? Sounding like he did? With the image of them kissing now solidly planted in her brain?

Impossible.

She breathed. Blinked a half dozen times or so. Her skin warmed even though she hadn't yet uttered the word *kiss*. Hell. There was not one portion of her being that didn't feel warm, from the inside out.

"Um. So, yeah. No snowman. No talking. And for the record, you might not initially think my request falls within the reasonable range, and I didn't think so last night when I first thought of it, but now I do. You…um… should know that."

He paused seconds before opening the door, stared down at her again and those green and amber eyes of his darkened to a burnished moss. The change wasn't fueled by anger or frustration or even confusion, because she saw desire looming in the depths of his gaze. As if he already knew what she was about to ask. As if he'd considered the very same.

Maybe he did know. Maybe he had.

"You're trouble," he said. "I knew it the second I saw you."

"Yeah? Well, you're trouble, too. But…I like it." Oh! Where had that come from? She blinked another half dozen times, breathed again. "I *might* like it."

"Tell me, Goldi," he said. "If I have to guess, I might guess wrong."

It was now or never. So, now please. "A kiss. I want you to kiss me."

His eyes darkened another full shade. She didn't know the word to describe their color now, but they pulled at her, made her want so much more than a kiss. But… she'd take the kiss and be happy with it. Maybe for the rest of her life.

A low growl emerged from the back of his throat. And that sound? The heat in her belly grew hotter, her shivers grew stronger.

"A kiss," she repeated firmly, with far more bravado than she felt. "A real kiss, Liam. Not just a peck on my cheek or forehead, but a full-blown, sweep-me-away type of a kiss." Oh, wow. She was both proud and shocked she'd said that so clearly.

His arms tightened around her at these words, and hunger entered his gaze.

That seemed so very positive, so she continued with, "I think a kiss is fair compensation for winning the Blizzard Championship and for almost dying for the second time in the span of a few days. Don't you?"

"Damn it, Goldi, I'm not made of stone," he said half under his breath. "Be careful what you ask for. I'm not a man to…have fantasies about or tie yourself to."

"I don't see a problem with a fantasy or two," she said, "and I'm not asking you for a diamond ring. Just a simple kiss." Her heart slammed against her breastbone and her mouth went dry. She was out of her mind. Absolutely so. But now that she'd started this, now that she saw and heard the same desire from Liam, she wasn't about to back off. "Well, maybe not a *simple* kiss. One amazing, toe-curling kiss. I think you might like it, too."

A glimmer of amusement swept over his features. "Toe-curling? Who talks like that?" He shoved open the door and carted her to the living room. But he did not set her down. He kept holding her, staring into her eyes, and yeah, that seemed positive, too. Very much so.

"My grandma did, so I guess I do, too."

"A kiss. You're asking for a kiss."

"Yes, please," she said. "Just make it—"

"Toe-curling, yeah." He closed his eyes, let out a sigh. "Can't say I'm entirely sure I know what that is, but it is your prize, after all. But who determines if it's toe-curling?"

"Well, me, of course," she said, further emboldened by his seeming acceptance of her proposal. "I'll have to be the judge. I mean, it's my toes you have to curl."

"Sounds painful. But okay, I'll…ah…"

"You'll what?" she prodded.

Another sigh. "This is a very bad idea. You know that, right?"

Oh, no. She couldn't let him think that through. Because, yes, it was a very bad idea. It was, at the exact same time, the best idea in the entire world. "Well, we could bet on that, as well," she said, her voice low. Breathless. And so unlike her normal voice. "If you're right and it turns out to be a bad idea, you can choose a prize. If I am right, then I get anoth—"

"Stop. No more talking." He carried her to the couch. "No more prizes."

"But I get this one, right?" Realizing he was about to deposit her on the sofa like an invalid, she stiffened in his arms. Nope. That was not going to happen. At least not before she got her kiss.

"Oh, no you don't, mister. I don't need to rest. I'm just fine. Well, maybe a little damp from the snow, but nothing that can't be fixed. Later. So, if you think you're going to plop me down and walk away after I've just asked you to kiss me, then you are strongly mistaken."

"Am I?"

"Yes. Strongly. I fell, yes, but I wasn't in the snow for long and—"

"Shh, Goldi. I can't kiss you when you're talking so much."

Oh. Well, then. "No more talking. I'll just…um… be quiet."

"Perfect." Still holding her, he sat down on the sofa. A second, then another, then another ten passed before he slowly helped her shift so she was sitting on his lap, facing him.

They were close. So freaking close. Eye to eye, nose to nose, almost lip to lip. And oh, how she yearned to stroke her fingers across the firm line of his jaw, up to his cheek, into his hair. But she didn't move, too afraid that he'd change his mind if she did anything other than wait. She couldn't bear it if he changed his mind. Now this kiss seemed of the highest priority. Over food and water and oxygen and sleep. It was all she wanted.

All she needed. Desired. Wished for. *Craved.*

"What are you doing to me, Goldi?"

"Probably the exact same thing you're doing to me."

"And that helps how?"

"Just kiss me, Liam. Please."

It must have been the please that did it, because the second the word slipped out, he groaned in a deep, almost guttural way, and in the space of half a heartbeat, his lips were on hers, pushing a soft moan from her throat.

His hands came to her waist and he brought her even closer as he deepened the kiss, his mouth firm, his hold secure. Curls of warmth trickled over her skin, suffused into her blood and seeped into her bones until nothing else existed. Except for them, his mouth on hers and friction and heat and want and need.

Just that quick. Just that effortlessly.

Made her want even more. She should've asked for an hour of kissing. Two hours. An entire night…the rest of her life. In this moment, that seemed reasonable. Necessary. Because she knew, really knew, that this kiss from this man would leave its mark. And she would never be the same. No matter how many miles she traveled or how many years passed.

Sliding his hands to the small of her back, he shifted them again, somehow bringing their bodies even closer together. Where did he start and she begin? She couldn't tell. Didn't know and didn't want to know. They were one.

His tongue pushed into her mouth, hungry and searching and demanding everything she could give, accepting nothing less. She opened her mouth and a moan, followed by another, whispered from the depths of her soul as she capitulated. Toe-curling? Yes.

Life changing? Yes, that too.

A frisson of fear swept in, momentarily overriding her desire. Not from the strength of her reaction, but from the knowledge that she would likely yearn for this man every day, in every way a woman could. The fallout of this action—a kiss—could be devastating. Somehow, more so than learning what she had about Rico. And that right there told her a hell of a lot.

She was already a goner. For Liam. A man she'd known for less than three days, yet her soul recognized from the moment she heard his voice. Her body recognized him, as well. Down to the bone, she knew this man. Oh, she didn't yet know the details that had built him, but she knew his heart. She knew his soul. She knew *him*. Had waited for him.

And here he was, kissing her, touching her, their bodies pressed together and nothing would ever be the same again.

Very purposely, she shoved the fear into a ball and pushed it as far down as possible. Whatever came next, whatever happened after this kiss? Well, she'd deal with it then. Later. When she had to. But she refused to allow her fears to weaken *this*.

Right now, he demanded her attention, her entire focus, and she wouldn't deny him the same pleasure he was giving her. So she returned his kiss with the same fervor, the same hunger, the same need and as she did, pushed her fingers into his hair and held on for dear life. Maybe, just maybe, if she held on, he wouldn't stop. He would just keep kissing her…forever.

As if he could read her thoughts, he groaned and wrapped his arms around her body and pulled back just enough for their lips to separate. She missed him instantly.

No. Not yet. Please not yet.

"Dangerous," he said, his lips so close to hers, yet not touching. "But irresistible."

Before she realized exactly what was happening, he scooped her up in his arms again and was heading toward the stairs that led to his bedroom. "Guess I like the danger because I'm taking you to bed. If you're not okay with that, you better say something."

"Yes. Yes, I am okay with that," she said. "So long as you are staying there with me."

"That would be my intent, Goldi. Just—"

"I am sure, Liam. I know what I want. Trust me on that, okay?"

One swift nod and he carried her upstairs with the same ease he had through the snow. When they reached his bedroom, he gently set her down on his bed.

Doubt entered his gaze, concern perhaps that this wasn't a good idea. And maybe it wasn't, but she wanted him, wanted this, and she didn't want Liam to think otherwise, not even for a second.

She lifted her sweatshirt over her head and tossed it on the floor. Unclasped her bra and took that off, tossed it in the same direction as the sweatshirt. And Liam? Whatever doubt had existed a mere second ago seemed to be gone, replaced by the need she'd witnessed earlier.

The same need she had. For him. For *them*.

"Help me with my jeans?" she asked. "Please?"

He came to her then without pause and unbuttoned her jeans, dragged them down and off her legs. Her panties were next, and there she lay, naked in front of this man.

Gently grasping her arms, he started to lean toward her, his view unmistakably on her breasts…but no. Not yet. With a teasing grin, she pushed him back and yanked at his sweatshirt. "You're still dressed," she said. "That's a problem."

"Is it now?"

"Mmm-hmm. New rule. No more touching until we get your clothes off," she said, feeling powerful and beautiful and…sexy. "I need to see you, Liam. Feel you, too."

"I think I can manage that." He removed his sweatshirt with the same speed that she had hers, and his jeans came off quicker than she would've imagined possible. And there *he* was, naked save his boxers, and oh, was he a sight to behold.

Strong. Muscular. Long and lean and—in this minute— all hers. All hers.

"Boxers," she whispered. "Don't forget those."

"Patience, woman, geez." But then, he did as she asked, and there was nothing between them, nothing to get in their way. "Happy now?"

"Very much so." Breathless. A mass of trembles. Needy. But yes, happy.

"Trouble," he repeated. Kneeling over, he brushed his thumb over one nipple and then the other, rubbing in small, soft circles that dragged yet another moan from her lips. "You're beautiful, Meredith. And you're killing me with those moans."

"I can stop."

"Ah. Don't. Stop."

His mouth captured hers for another long, searing kiss, igniting this desperate, consuming need another degree.

Melting…she was melting. There really wasn't another way to state what was happening. From her bones to her skin, she became a puddle beneath Liam's touch. Beneath his hands and his mouth and his body. She became his, just as he became hers.

She lifted her hips, wrapped her legs around his torso and ran her hands down the warm length of his back.

All to show him that she was ready and that there wasn't any reason to wait.

But he had other ideas. "We're not there yet, sweetheart," he said, lifting his mouth from hers. "Not yet. We have all day. All night. Why would we rush this?"

Oh. Well, then. "Okay. No hurry."

Time disappeared into a vacuum. Five minutes, ten, three days, she no longer knew or cared. In this space of untraceable time, he skimmed his fingers down her stomach, to her thighs and then followed that very same path with his mouth. Tasting. Tickling. Teasing.

And as he did, her body came to life in an engulfing rush of shivering need, greater even than before, which hadn't seemed possible. She ached for him intensely.

Viscerally. And regardless of what he'd said, she didn't believe she could hold out for much longer.

"Now, Liam. Please," she begged. "I can't wait. I need you inside of me."

"Oh, now, for a woman who fought against a snowstorm and survived? Pretty sure you can do anything you set your mind to," he said with a quirky, teasing smile. "Besides which, I don't think I'm quite done exploring your body yet."

She gave him another minute, maybe two, before reaching the decision that if he could torture her, she could certainly return the favor. She rolled out from beneath him and pushed him down, flat on his back with a lot less effort than it should've taken. Maybe he was melting too? A distinct possibility. "Now, it is my turn."

"Oh, is it?" he asked with a smile born of pure anticipation. Excitement was there, too, along with that desire and heat. "Well, if you're sure, I won't object."

"I insist." Lightly—ever so lightly—she trailed her fingers up his arms to his shoulders, leaned forward and brushed her hair across his chest, eliciting a delicious-sounding sigh. And that sound resonated just as strongly, just as deeply as what she experienced, with how he made her feel. Like he had done with her, she used her tongue to taste, to explore.

And everywhere she touched, his skin warmed, muscles tensed and released and then tensed and released again.

Yes.

Giving him pleasure was just as—if not more—satisfying than receiving pleasure. She kissed his chest, his stomach. He wove his fingers into her hair as she did, as she continued downward to his hips and his thighs, his hands tightening incrementally as she licked and tasted and pleasured and…loved.

Slowly, she crawled her way back up his body, one enticing inch at a time, to kiss him fully on the lips.

"You win," Liam said against her mouth as he gripped her waist. She did not object. She did not mind winning this particular battle in any way whatsoever. Together, they rolled, switching places. "No more waiting. No more teasing. You're going to kill me if this keeps up."

Oh. Here they were. *Now.* "If I remember correctly, you started the temptation game."

"You weren't supposed to turn the tables."

"Well, guess you have more to learn about me."

"Maybe I do."

The talking stopped again as he kissed her hard and then looked straight into her eyes as she opened her legs to him, for him.

He entered her in one long slide that, yes, stole whatever breath she had remaining clean from her lungs. And his eyes, hooded and dark and intense and beautiful, remained locked with hers. As if he couldn't bear to turn away.

Connected as one and so freaking intimate.

His hips moved against hers, over and over. She wrapped her legs tightly around him and pushed him in deeper. And then deeper still. Their bodies merged in perfect synchronicity, and Meredith gave herself to the sensations, lost in the power of the moment, in the pleasure swimming through her blood.

And all the while, Liam's gaze never left hers even for a millisecond. She kept her gaze on his, too, in the hopes she would remember every second of this encounter. Because forever and a day from now, she wanted to be able to pull it to her memory and see it exactly as she saw it now. Feel everything she felt now.

Impossible, of course, but she had to try. Had to.

Friction. Heat. Desire. All right here, all for the taking. The pleasure built and built and built and built some more, and then all at once, every sensation gathered into a tight ball, pulsated once…twice…three times before she gave up the fight.

She moaned and pushed herself against Liam, taking him as far as she could while the truest form of pleasure rippled and flowed through her body. This was…beautiful and sexy and somehow pure.

It was what was supposed to be. She believed this. She knew this.

Liam's body tensed, stilled and then he drove into her again as he found his release. His hands came to her arms, and he held on tight as he shuddered, as his eyelids drooped and one more long, satisfied groan rumbled from his throat.

Collapsing on top of her, he rested his head on her breasts, ran his fingers down her arms and together they lay there, still entwined.

Still one.

She wondered if he knew they belonged together. And if he didn't yet know this, if he would eventually come to the same conclusion. Because she was, without doubt, his. And he was, also without doubt, hers. Knowing what she did about this man, it might take him a while to figure this out, but she would wait. She would be patient. She would…

Do exactly as she had with Rico? Keep herself open and available in the hopes that he'd one day show up at her door, announce his love and carry her away?

Oh. Lord. No. She couldn't allow herself to fall into

old patterns just as she was trying to find her own way in this world.

Meredith kissed Liam's shoulder, and while she didn't say anything, her soul mourned. Her heart broke. Because she wouldn't wait like she had with Rico. Not for years. She wouldn't do that to herself again, for anyone.

Even for the man she'd dreamed of. Even for the man she knew she belonged with. Even for the man who had just shown her more than she'd ever seen.

Her life was valuable. And she intended on living it, whether Liam was at her side or not.

So she would give him a little time, because she also knew he would need some. Demons of one sort or another raged a battle in his brain, his heart, and she couldn't do anything other than allow him some space to win that war. If he chose to fight it.

But if he didn't… If days melted into weeks, weeks into months, she'd force open her eyes, accept the truth and just live her life. If that happened, would she ever stop hoping?

Eventually, yes. Eventually. The question left unanswered was the precise length of "eventually." Maybe, if she were very lucky, she wouldn't have to find out.

Chapter Nine

Liam waited for Meredith to fasten her seat belt before he closed the passenger's side door. It was midafternoon the next day, and while common sense dictated waiting until tomorrow to take her to her friend's house in Steamboat Springs proper, his heart needed her gone posthaste. Before he dragged her to bed and had his way with her again. It shouldn't have happened once. Or twice, later last night. Or…well, didn't matter how many times.

He couldn't let it happen again.

What had occurred between them would stay in his memory for a long while to come, because frankly, he'd never experienced anything like he had with his Goldilocks.

Not even with Christy. A realization that both stunned and shamed him. No one should be able to hold a candle next to the woman he married. Yet, somehow, this woman had. And that made him feel like a heel.

His thoughts hadn't turned that route until this morning, when he woke with Meredith curled against him, her hair in his nose and their bodies spooned. Initially, he'd felt joy and satisfaction and hope. Initially, he'd had the wild idea of asking her to stay.

But she'd slept for a while in his arms, and as she did, thoughts of his wife returned.

That was when the guilt set in, quickly followed by all those logical reasons why he was better off alone. Far better to trust in decisions that had already proven beneficial and solid than it was to blindly grab at a smoky, fog-covered dream that held zero substance.

By the time Meredith awakened, his resolve had become steel. An awkward type of intimacy had set in. There was no denying what they had experienced, and he hadn't yet figured out how to talk to her about any of it. She couldn't have expectations. He needed to be sure she realized this, yet…like always, he despised hurting this woman's feelings.

There was also a profound sense of emptiness that had set in.

Nothing new. He'd felt that way before, had combatted that emptiness with work and then later with Fiona and Cassie and eventually with Max and Maggie. He could certainly beat away that emptiness again. The doing shouldn't be nearly as difficult this time. There wasn't a comparison to saying goodbye to a woman he'd only just met and the woman he'd planned on spending the entirety of his life with.

Or there shouldn't be.

Max and Maggie pushed at his heels, waiting for him to open the door to the back seat of his truck, knowing they were going for a ride. He did and they jumped in, tails wagging.

At the driver's door, he paused, breathed in the cool air and tried to let the serenity of the mountains, of his home, seep into his blood and calm the churning storm. Didn't work. Not yet, anyway.

But it would. Once he was on his own again.

He slid into his seat, forced a smile in Meredith's direction as he put the truck into Drive. He tried not to notice the tense set of her shoulders, the stubborn lift of her chin. Tried not to give in to this instinct to reach over, pull her into his arms and beg her to stay. Offer the world if she'd only stay with him and his dogs here on his mountain. Lord, that temptation was strong, but he resisted. Had to. For her, for him. For his sanity and well-being.

Hers, too, as far as that went.

"Bet you're happy to finally see your friend, huh?" He turned the truck around and headed down the slope of his driveway, taking care to go slow. "Sorry there isn't phone service yet, but I bet you'll have a signal on your iPhone soon enough. Can check in with her, then. Let her know you're safe and sound and on your way."

She held up her phone and nodded with an equally forced smile. "I'm ready."

"Hey," he said, turning onto the road, "do you remember where your car is? Might be able to get your luggage if you do. Would be nice to have your stuff back, right?"

"It wasn't far down this road, just after that first hill and curve, but…I don't know if I can remember the exact spot. I would like my clothes, if it isn't too hard to find the car. Just don't want you to go out of your way," she said quietly. "You've done more than your fair share."

"Well, let's see what we can do. Try to remember the best you can and tell me when to stop." What he didn't say, what he barely admitted to himself, is that he would do almost anything for this woman. Almost. "Maybe we'll luck out."

They did indeed luck out. Her car wasn't that far off the road, but getting to it would take a fair amount of effort.

He told her to wait for him in the truck—he didn't want to see her fall again—and he kept the dogs there, too. For company. And as he made his way through the snow, he couldn't help but think of her on that night, with the storm raging, all alone and lost and…terrified. He'd known since she'd told him the story that she could've died out here by herself, and he'd felt for her, had been damn glad Max and Maggie had come to the rescue.

But now a different type of terror took hold. He could've lost her before he'd ever even known she existed. And while there wasn't a lick of sense in his next thought, he couldn't rid himself of it, either: he hadn't been there to protect her when she needed protecting.

Ripped him to shreds thinking of that, again, with another woman he…well, cared about. Strongly.

When he arrived at the car and saw the open suitcase in the back seat, clothes strewn about, he could almost see her, panicking and dressing herself in the layers he found her in, scared and gathering her courage, her strength, to do what she needed.

It amazed him, really.

Hurriedly, he shoved the loose clothing back into her suitcase, latched it tight and went back the way he came, toward his truck, his dogs and Goldi. He'd ask her for the rental information, so he could call the company and tell them where the car was located. It wasn't a lot, but he wanted to take that weight off her shoulders since he couldn't reverse time and save her from the ordeal to begin with. But yeah, he would if he could.

He tossed the suitcase in the back seat with the dogs, smiled at Goldi who had pivoted to see him. "Got it," he said. "Not a problem, and now you're all set."

"Yes," she said, somewhat faintly. "All set. Thank you, Liam."

"Welcome."

A minute later, they were once again driving toward Steamboat Springs in silence. Painful silence.

But hell, he didn't know what to say. Didn't have a clue as to how to explain everything in his head and heart. Didn't know. But he wished he did. Wished he had the words to tell this woman that she had affected him deeply but that his life and future were set. And why. Yeah, he really wished he could tell her the whys. That, he knew, was out of the question.

He didn't speak of Christy or their child. Didn't utter a word of his loss. To anyone.

"Talk to me," he said, somewhat gruffly. "You're too quiet."

"Oh, my," she said with a hint of her old, spunky, adorable self. "I'm too quiet and you're asking me to talk? Did *you* fall and bonk your head out there?"

"No, I just…like hearing your voice." Oh, hell. Where had that come from? "And it will be slowgoing for a bit here, might as well have a conversation. Right?"

"Sure. What would you like to talk about?"

"How about your plans, once everything settles again?" Like how long was she planning on sticking around Steamboat Springs? And did he want to know so he could avoid her or so he could find her? "You never mentioned how long this visit was meant to last."

"Anywhere from a few weeks to open-ended. I'm not really sure yet. Will depend on…well, several factors that remain unknown." Meredith shrugged and closed the heating vent nearest her. "As to my plans, those are rather loose, too. Rachel and I have a lot to catch up on, and I've never met her husband. We'll start with that, I guess, and see where we end up."

"Gotcha. Why…ah, did you quit your job?" He just wanted her to talk. Didn't much care about the topic. Just needed to keep hearing her voice. "Feel like sharing?"

"Oh. Well, that's a long story. Are you sure you're up for it?"

"Yup. I will listen to anything you want to share."

"Okay, then," she said. "I can't remember if I already told you, but I grew up in a wealthy family. We never lacked for anything. But my parents—and they're wonderful people, really, so please don't think they aren't—have a view of the world that they wanted me and my brothers to have. So, we were…what's a good word? Sheltered, yes, but also shown our paths from early on. The paths they decided we were meant to take. And that was that."

She continued to talk, weaving the story of her life for Liam's benefit. How her parents formed decisions for her, their expectations, her desperate want to make them proud even above her own happiness.

He hated that. Hated that she ever gave up even a second of what would make her happy for another person's benefit. It didn't surprise him, though. Not in the least. It was the way this woman was built.

Kind. Caring. Giving. To a fault.

"I met Rico in college, and with him, I suddenly no longer cared about what my parents wanted or thought. Love," she said with a sarcastic edge. "I thought we were in love."

The rest of her tale came out in a short, succinct manner. There wasn't a lick of emotion in Meredith's voice, but Liam recognized her hurt, her numbing shock, at learning how she'd gotten her job and what had really occurred with this man she'd believed loved her. And frankly, he wanted to punch both her father and this Rico square in the jaw.

For hurting this woman. She should never be hurt or betrayed. By anyone.

She wrapped up the story by saying, "So that is why I quit my job. What brought me here, to Steamboat Springs. I am determined to figure out my life without anyone else's interference. From here on out. My life, my choices and…well, I guess that's it."

"That was a lot, Goldi. And I'm proud of you." He was. Massively so.

"Thank you. I…it's time, I guess. Nothing more, nothing less."

"Right. I agree." Now what? "My parents died when I was a kid," he said, shocking himself. Where had that come from? And *why*? He didn't want to talk about that. Did he? "Doesn't matter, I guess. It was a long time ago. Not sure why I brought it up."

"Probably because some part of you wants to talk about it, and I am more than happy to listen." He felt more than saw that she angled herself toward him, and he could clearly imagine the look of compassion and sorrow decorating her features. "Maybe we're just finishing our conversation from yesterday, when you told me you were raised in Florida with your grandfather. I wondered then how that happened. I'm guessing this is why?"

"Yup. After our parents' deaths, Fiona went to live with my mother's sister. Neither our grandfather or our aunt had the room for both of us, but I know it was a tough decision for them. They hated separating us. They—" Liam cleared his throat "—made sure we spent holidays and summers together, though. Every year. So, that was good. Not the same, but good."

"No, not the same." A heavy sigh, as if she were imagining how that might have affected Liam and Fiona. As if the facts of his childhood somehow hurt *her*. "I'm so sorry. What happened? Your parents must have been pretty young still, right?"

He didn't want to answer. Yet, he did. Since he'd broached the topic, he figured he'd keep talking. Was only fair. More to the point, he couldn't ignore the sudden desire to let her in, to show her just a sliver of his foundation. Just a little, mind you. Not too much.

"Well, yeah, they were," he said, taking a careful right onto a cross street. The roads weren't in great shape. He should've waited until tomorrow for this drive for safety. "It was their anniversary. They went out for an early dinner, and with the sitter's help, Fiona and I baked a cake. It was rather ugly, actually, but we wanted to surprise them when they came home. Fiona drew a bunch of pictures, and we hung those around the living room."

"Sounds perfect. How old were you?"

He cleared his throat again. "I was ten. Fiona was seven."

"So young."

"Yeah. Anyway," Liam said, now wanting to get through the telling of this particular story as quickly as possible, "our plan was to hide when they came home, jump out just as they opened the door and show them the cake we'd made. They…ah, never made it home. It was raining that night, pretty hard. I remember the sound of it hitting the roof, the windows of our house. Found out later that Dad took a curve too fast, lost control of the Jeep." Here, he stopped. He hadn't thought about this for most of his adult life. "The car went down a ravine, rolled and crashed at the bottom. We…ah, didn't even know what happened until the next day."

Meredith's hand came to his thigh, and the weight and the warmth and the woman behind the touch offered comfort. Security. Understanding. "Oh, Liam," she said, her voice soft. Soothing. "I guess I'm not sure what to say, other than how sorry I am for you and your sister."

"Thank you. The ravine was steep," he continued, unsure why he felt the need to say more. But he did, so he did. "Even so, they probably would've survived if they'd worn their seat belts. Can't figure that one out, because they always did when we were all in the car together. As it was, Mom died pretty much instantly. Dad followed a few days later."

He waited for another "I'm sorry" and all the typical platitudes that people gave in moments such as these. Oh, he didn't doubt that Meredith would mean every last one, but they always came across—to Liam—as somewhat shallow. What a person said when they didn't know what else to say, how to react, how to really be there for someone else.

He supposed that was why they called them platitudes, and that was fine. No one had to be there for him. He had all he needed. All he ever would need.

A minute or two of silence passed. Then, "Did you still eat the cake?" she asked in a somber tone, surprising him clear through.

Why? He should've known better than to expect the typical from Goldi. Nothing about her fell into the ordinary range. "I think I would've smashed it on the floor, tossed it out the back door, threw it against a wall. I don't know. Something."

Those words, the vehemence behind them, struck

deeply. She was right on the money. They *had* destroyed the cake, two days later, but in the sink. Water from the faucet running at full blast and two angry, distraught children wielding wooden spoons. They'd kept at it—Fiona crying and Liam stone silent—until the cake had become mush and most of it had gone down the drain. "Curious, Goldi. Why that question? Why do you think you'd behave in that way?"

She squeezed his thigh lightly. "Because the cake was made to be a happy surprise, a gift and a celebration to have with your parents. I would think that learning what had happened, that they were never coming home, would never see what you and sister had done for them out of love, would've made that cake…I don't know, an enemy, I guess? I would need to demolish the cake." She shook her head, sighed. "Not sure if that makes sense."

"More than you know." She'd nailed it. And why was he surprised? "And that is what we did, and for about an hour afterward, we felt a hell of a lot better."

Until, of course, they realized that cake or no cake didn't change their reality or their sadness or their loss. Their parents were gone. They couldn't escape that.

"Thank you for sharing," she said. "I know that wasn't easy for you." Were those tears he heard in her voice? Maybe. Probably. She was that way. "But I am honored you did."

"It was a long time ago." Emotion lodged in his throat. He pushed it down deep, just as he always did. "I wouldn't have shared if I didn't want to. So there's that."

"Right. There's that." A small laugh. "I can still be grateful and honored."

"I suppose you can."

A silent calm enveloped the interior of the truck, and

Liam no longer felt the need for either of them to talk. The quiet soothed, connected. It was the same sensation that his solitary lifestyle in the mountains offered. He didn't question or analyze why—his stance on that and Meredith hadn't altered—but he allowed himself to accept the peace. Allowed himself to accept that, for whatever reason, this woman soothed the beast inside.

"Oh!" she said, breaking his concentration. "I have a signal! Let me call Rachel."

So she did, and he continued to drive. The squeal from the other side of the phone was easily heard from his position, as was Meredith's explanation of what had transpired after her plane had landed: getting lost, her accident, her unusual rescue and that she was on her way to Rachel's and should be there soon, but no, she didn't know exactly how long it would take.

To that, he said, "Within twenty to thirty minutes, I'm guessing. Roads are getting better the closer we get to town, and we're…almost there." Almost. There.

Why hadn't he waited another day?

"Thank you, Liam," Meredith said before repeating the information to her friend. The two talked for another five minutes or so before she disconnected the call. "People were looking for me. I guess Cole's brother, Reid, is a ski patroller, so he apparently knows the mountains even better than you! He and his friends have been on the search since yesterday."

"I'm not surprised. I'm just glad they didn't have anything to find, because that would've meant you weren't safe." Again, a kick of nausea hit his stomach. "You should know I despise that thought. Be more careful in the future, Meredith, okay? Stay safe."

"Oh, trust me, I don't plan on anything like that ever happening again."

"Of course, you don't. But come on, Goldi, you didn't plan on that, either," he said. "Which is what I'm talking about. If you're going into a new area, do your research. Know where you'll be, figure out more than one path to get you there and make damn sure you have a backup plan. I—that is, my dogs—won't be around. Gotta count on yourself."

"Why, Liam," she said. "You sound concerned. That's sweet."

Concerned? More like out of his mind with gut-wrenching worry that she'd get herself in another predicament and he wouldn't be there, couldn't be there, to help. "Just some solid, practical advice that you should take to heart. Danger doesn't typically announce itself."

"I realize that. And yes, of course, I will take more care in the future."

"Good." Then, trying to lighten the moment, he said, "Don't make me hire a team of bodyguards to follow you around. Take care of yourself, that's all I ask."

"And I already agreed."

Maggie took that moment to wedge her head over the back of the seat and laid it on Meredith's shoulder. Max followed suit with her other shoulder, and in that strange canine unison the two had, they whined. Loudly. Voicing their unhappiness, their own concern, at the possibility of Meredith being in danger again? Wouldn't surprise him. More likely though, the dogs had somehow sensed they were about to lose their new friend.

Snuggling into the dog-head embrace, Meredith said, "It's okay, guys. I'll be fine! Maybe instead of body-guards, you two can just follow me around. I would… like that."

"They would, too," Liam admitted just as they offi-cially entered Steamboat Springs. "Read me your friend's address again? From what I remember, her house isn't too far."

Meredith did, and yeah, another few minutes of her company was all he had left.

"Thank you, Liam."

"For?"

"Everything. Just…everything." She breathed in quickly, sharply. "This is odd, isn't it? I feel as if I've known you for far longer than a few days, and we're about to say…goodbye?"

"You're welcome, and yeah, I know what you mean." He didn't miss that she'd ended that sentence as a question, rather than a statement, and that meant she was curious if they'd see each other again.

Logical, with how they'd spent last night. He had to give her something. Not just an answer, but some type of understanding of what she'd come to mean to him, because it was the truth. And she deserved that. *They* deserved that. But words were not his strong suit, and he still hadn't figured out how to say all that should be said.

"I'll be around. And Meredith? Thank you, too. I've… enjoyed these days with you. Please don't doubt that."

"Okay. I…I won't. Thank you."

Not enough. Not nearly enough. But it was all he had. Probably was all he'd ever have.

Whether it be the mood or something undefined, Max and Maggie began whining again in long, serious notes of dismay. Hell. Knowing Liam's luck, they'd do the same all the way home in their distress over losing Meredith, likely increasing in volume with each mile driven.

And, hell, again. With how fiercely his heart ached now while the woman remained sitting next to him, he might just join them. Because yeah, this might be the right—the only—action to take, he despised the idea as much as his dogs seemed to. Unlike his shepherds, though, he knew what was best.

And this, regardless of how much the loss burned in his gut, was best.

Sitting up in bed, Meredith stretched her arms and yawned. Looked around the guest room she was staying in at Rachel's and yawned again. It would be a long day. Longer than yesterday, which had been longer than the day before.

Her third day with Rachel. Her third mostly sleepless night in a row. All due to Liam. She couldn't stop thinking about him. Wondering what he was doing. If he was missing her with the same strength she missed him.

Obviously not. He knew where to find her and he hadn't come looking.

When they'd arrived here together, he'd given her this long, searching look, a quick hug and then without a backward glance, had driven off. Literally into the sunset.

Fortunately, she hadn't had the time to think too hard on that until later that night, when she'd finally fallen into this bed. First, there had been hugs from Rachel and her husband, Cole. Next, she'd had the difficult phone calls to make to her family, which had been emotional and supportive.

Her father had wanted to fly out there immediately, when he'd learned she was missing in a snowstorm, but Rachel had convinced him to wait until the storm cleared. Until they had more information.

Surprising that he'd capitulated, but he had. She didn't think he'd have waited a lot longer, though. For a man who was used to getting what he wanted when he wanted,

Arthur Jensen had shown incredible restraint. But he'd been scared. She heard it in his voice.

And when he apologized for cutting her communication from the family, she almost cried. Probaby would've if Rachel and Cole hadn't been nearby.

Not even once had he mentioned that she wouldn't have been in that predicament to begin with if she hadn't made the decision she had, to go out on her own. He even said he was proud of her, for sticking to her guns. They had a lot more to talk about, but she felt sure they would repair their relationship and that he finally understood her need to find independence. She hoped so anyway.

The remainder of the day had been spent with Rachel, drinking wine and catching up, learning about all the gaps in each other's lives. They'd stayed up so late, had giggled so hard, that Cole—who had tried to turn in hours earlier—finally gave up the fight and joined them.

A pleasant night. Except, of course, for missing Liam.

Yesterday had been much the same: more talking, more laughing and a quick tour around Steamboat Springs. They'd eaten lunch at Cole's family's restaurant, Foster's Pub and Grill, and she'd had the opportunity to meet both of his brothers, Reid and Dylan, and his sister, Haley.

What hadn't happened, what she thought was on the agenda for today, was the reason she came here in the first place: to think about her future, determine what that might look like, with Rachel as a sounding board. A difficult proposition from the beginning, but meeting Liam had made that even more difficult. A future. Her future. With or without Liam?

Standing, Meredith made the bed and grabbed a change of clothes, went to the log cabin's bathroom and took a shower. Mostly cold, to wake up her tired brain.

Even with missing Liam, she couldn't deny the pleasure of being here with Rachel, especially after so long. And oh, she seemed happy, living in this house with her handsome husband. Such a different life her friend had chosen from that in which she'd been raised.

While the log cabin was gorgeous, it wasn't a large home by any stretch of the imagination. Two bedrooms. One bathroom. Dollhouse-sized when compared to what Rachel had grown up with, to what *Meredith* had grown up with. But yes, she could see being happy in a place like this, with a love like her friend had so fortunately found. Deliriously so, even. Except in her head, it was Liam's face and his mountain cabin that she saw.

Damn that man anyway.

"'I'll be around,'" she mimicked as she towel-dried her legs. "'I've enjoyed these days with you. Please don't doubt that.'"

With any other man, she would have instantly taken those words as a brush-off. Would've instantly felt taken advantage of, even though she'd walked into their love-making knowing how it could, probably would, end.

But with Liam?

She didn't believe he'd just coldly brush her off, as if she wasn't anything more than a one-night stand. No, what she believed was that he was confused and didn't know how to handle the situation. That he had done the best he could. But that she meant something to him, something important, and that maybe he just hadn't reconciled himself with that yet.

The possibility also existed that she had finally reached the delusional stage and her brain refused to accept the truth. Or her heart. Or both.

She'd give him time. She'd wait it out for a little while

before deciding on the delusional, blind and naive love-sick choice.

Dressing in a pair of jeans and a long, butter-yellow sweater, Meredith brushed her damp hair and rolled it into a clip on top of her head. The scent of coffee and cinnamon wafted through the closed door as she finished her morning routine. Rachel and Cole must be awake.

She found them both in the kitchen, sitting at the table over their coffee, chatting easily.

They were quite the attractive pair. Rachel with her long, straight blond hair and wide blue eyes and Cole with his black hair and dark brown eyes. And whenever they looked at each other, you'd have to be in a coma not to see the love they had each for other.

Beautiful. Something to aim for someday.

"Morning," she said with a smile. "That coffee smells amazing."

"Thank Cole," Rachel said. "I was out early this morning. But those cinnamon rolls you smell? All me, I'll have you know. And they're just about warmed up, so hope you're hungry."

"Morning to you, Meredith." Cole stood and poured her a cup of coffee, which he brought back to the table. "Don't believe a word my wife says. Those rolls came from a coffeehouse called the Beanery and were baked by the owner, our friend, Lola. You'll love them. I guarantee you've never tasted any as good."

"Hrmph. I said they were almost done warming, not that I baked them with my own two hands, and I bought them, didn't I?" Rachel wrinkled her nose in Cole's direction. "But he is right. They're delicious and I thought they'd be the perfect start to our day."

"You guys are already like an old married couple. It's cute." And even this friendly, warmhearted bickering brought about a yearning. Geez. She was a mess. "And I am hungry, so can't wait to try Lola's famous cinnamon rolls."

She did a few minutes later, over light conversation about the weather—which was, thankfully, back to normal for this time of year—and an upcoming baby shower for their sister-in-law, Chelsea, who was married to Cole's brother, Dylan. Mostly, Meredith just listened, enjoying the camaraderie between husband and wife. How effortless they were together, from their speech to their body language to those intimate smiles they so often exchanged.

Yes, Rachel had found her nirvana. And from their conversations the past few days, Meredith knew it hadn't come easily. She and Cole had to work for this, and okay, some of their choices fell into the questionable range, but they had done the best they could and their path brought them to this table, in this house, sharing coffee and cinnamon rolls and intimate smiles.

Could make a person believe that anything was possible.

"Okay, ladies, I'm due at work," Cole said, standing. In addition to the restaurant, his family also owned a sporting goods store, which he managed. He smiled at Meredith before kissing his wife. Then, "I should be home around seven, I think. I'll bring dinner."

Rachel's eyes followed him until he vanished down the hallway. When the sound of the front door closing reached their ears, she jumped from the table and grabbed a notebook and pen from the counter. Back in her seat, she flipped open to the first page and pushed it with the pen across the surface of the table to Meredith, saying, "Here. Let's see what we can figure out."

Picking up the pen, Meredith twisted it between her

fingers. "Yes. It's time. The practical should come first. What type of job I want and then the job itself. A place to live."

"Well, maybe we should begin with location? Seems that should come first, right?" Tapping her pink-painted nails against the table, Rachel said, "Do you want a completely fresh start, or are you thinking of staying in San Francisco since you still have your apartment?"

"The lease expires in two months." Good question. "So that isn't a huge issue. I have enough in savings to deal with that and probably a couple of months of expenses." She should give that money back to her father, really. She only had it due to his interference and help with her salary, but...that suddenly seemed of such little consequence.

Her goal was a whole new life. If she needed some help from her old life to make that happen, why not take it? And without her savings, she had...zero money. So, okay.

"Want to stay on the West Coast? Or try something different?"

"I am going to stay here, in Steamboat Springs." Meredith said the words before she'd even thought them through, but once she had, she knew that was the only choice she could make.

Oh, she still didn't plan on waiting for Liam for years, like she had with Rico. But...she couldn't be far away from him just yet, either. Yes. This was the right decision. Besides which, "You live here, Rach. I'd rather start over with my best friend close by than in a strange city all by myself."

She didn't talk about Liam. Wasn't ready to share her feelings on him just yet.

"Yes! I was hoping you'd come to that conclusion. I've

missed you!" Rachel's smile stretched from ear to ear. "And you know, you can stay here as long as you need. Don't feel as if you have to move out anytime soon. I like having you around."

"Aw, thank you. I like being around you, too, and I certainly won't be moving out in the next week. Depends on how long it takes me to find a job."

On the notebook, Meredith wrote the number *1*, which she circled, and next to it: *Live in Steamboat Springs*. Such a simple yet complex decision. Making it felt positive. Like the exactly right first step.

On a slippery, treacherous slope, perhaps. One that could cause her more harm than slamming into a tree and almost freezing to death. But oh, the possibilities—the reality of her dream—were endless. Beautiful. *Her* nirvana. *Her* happy ending. With Liam.

"Actually, I have an idea on the job front," Rachel was saying as she refilled her coffee cup. "Didn't want to bring it up until I knew what you were thinking about location."

"Yeah? What sort of a job?"

"The same sort you were doing in San Francisco. This is a vacation town, you know. Plenty of homes need staging. With your experience, you shouldn't have too much trouble getting a door to open. Relatively quickly, I'd imagine, and without your dad's help."

Well. If that were the case, she had to believe that her heart, that fate, had led her in the exact right direction. Now, she just had to keep walking. Keep following this path she was on and see what existed beyond the next bend in the road.

Chapter Ten

One week. Two weeks. Three weeks. Time just kept on ticking away, and it didn't friggin' matter if Liam was at home, working, outside, inside or asleep, that damn ache in his chest hadn't let loose for a millisecond since dropping Goldi off at her friend's place. That never-ending ache gave him pause, made him rethink what he shouldn't.

Hell. He'd even started listening to ABBA. "Mamma Mia," in particular.

And today he'd had enough. He *had* to see her, or try to, even if the doing was about the stupidest action he could take. First, though, he had to get through this meal with Fiona and Cassie.

His sister had phoned that morning, told him that enough was enough and to get his butt over there, or she'd barge into his sanctuary and wouldn't leave for a week.

She meant it, too. She'd done it before.

So here he was, with Fiona and Cassie, eating pot roast and vegetables on Sunday afternoon, trying to behave like a normal man instead of one hovering on the brink of insanity. He'd probably fooled his niece, but with the questioning looks his sister was directing his way? Nah, he hadn't fooled Fiona. She might not know what the problem was, but she'd honed in that there *was* a problem. Unlikely he'd get out of here without giving her a few answers.

"Will you be able to come see me in the Christmas play?" Cassie, who was cuter than any kid had the right to be, asked over a mouthful of mashed potatoes. "Please?"

It never failed to amaze Liam how much she looked like Fiona, with her light, strawberry-blond hair and vivid green eyes. Folks who didn't know better automatically assumed the two were mother and daughter and were astounded when they learned the truth, that Cassie was Fiona's foster daughter. Fiona was trying to change that, trying to untangle all the red tape to adopt Cassie, who had been in her care for the past three years.

Unfortunately, there was a lot of red tape.

"Wait a minute? It's barely November," Liam said. "There's already a Christmas play in the works? And of course, I will attend. Wouldn't miss it for the world, kiddo."

"She's a little ahead of herself," Fiona said, smiling at her daughter. "But there's always a Christmas play, and she's hoping to be one of the angels this year."

"Can't think of anyone better." Plate now empty, Liam pushed it back some and finished his milk. Always milk at Fiona's table if Cassie was present. It amused him, having such a rule. "You'll be a beautiful angel, so they'd be crazy not to make you one."

Joy lit up the girl's eyes. "I can't wait! Christmas is my favorite holiday."

"Better than Halloween? What about your birthday?" he teased. "Say it isn't so!"

"Christmas has carols and presents and cookies and a tree with sparkling lights and Santa Claus and Frosty the Snowman and…and…lots of other wonderful stuff," Cassie said in a matter-of-fact, what-are-you-crazy sort of way. "'Course it's better. Cookies, Uncle Liam!"

A rumble of a laugh burst from his lungs. He loved his family. Thank the good Lord that Fiona was on top of keeping them together; otherwise he and his loner self would miss these moments. "Can't argue with that. Cookies are right up there on the top of any list."

The dogs, who had been plopped on the floor in between his chair and Cassie's, recognized the word *cookies* and leaped to their feet, instantly on the lookout. For the past three weeks, they'd spent more time pacing the living room and sniffing the sofa that had been Goldi's bed than doing anything else. They were morose. Seemingly lost without her.

Here, in a place she had never been, they were doing better. Made him think he should leave them here for a while to give them some relief. But he'd miss them, and then he'd be completely alone in missing Goldi. The thought didn't sit well at all, so he nixed it.

Misery loved company and all of that.

The rest of dinner was a mix of quiet and Cassie chatter as they ate, with his niece talking about school, her new music teacher—who was, apparently, *amazing* and *funny* and *beautiful*—and, naturally, a good deal more about Christmas and the play and being an angel.

At the end of the meal, Fiona asked Cassie, "Did you finish your homework from Friday yet? If not, please do that before any television or phone calls or anything else. Deal?"

"Deal! And it's almost all done. Just have to practice my spelling words."

"Why don't you do that and I'll quiz you later?" Clearing the dishes, Fiona directed a look at Liam. "You can help me before you scurry back to your hidey-hole."

"Sure," he said. "I'm happy to be interrogated…help. I meant, I'm happy to help."

"What's *interrogated* mean?" Cassie was already halfway out of the dining room.

"To be relentlessly questioned," Liam answered as he, too, began clearing the dishes. "But I am just teasing. Go do your schoolwork. I'll say goodbye before I leave."

Hearing Cassie climb the stairs to her bedroom, Fiona turned her green-eyed, all-seeing gaze on Liam. "So, what is going on? And don't tell me nothing, because I'm smarter than that and have known you my entire life. You can't hide from me."

"You know," Liam said lightly, "one would almost think you're the older sibling, rather than the younger. Bossing me around like that! Why, I swear I remember this sweet, quiet little girl who used to trail after me and listen to every word I said as if it were gospel."

"Oh, I remember those days, too. And then we grew up." She went to the kitchen, where she started rinsing the dishes. "Are you okay? Tell me that much, at least."

"Honestly, Fi? I don't know." And then, for the second time in less than a month, he opened up to another person. Sure, this was his sister and not the woman who'd managed to carve herself into his heart, but still. He talked, she listened and he finished with, "So, yeah. This woman shows up at my house out of nowhere and…I don't know. I might miss her."

"You love her," Fiona said without missing a beat or mincing words. "Only other time I've seen you like this, heard you like this, was when you met Christy. And yes, you miss this woman. Doesn't really matter how long you've known a person if love is involved. And when you love someone and haven't seen them in close to a month, you tend to miss them."

"Love? I did not say—"

Fiona patted his arm. "That's because you haven't admitted it to yourself yet, and that's just fine. You don't have to admit anything until you're ready to. But I can see the truth on your face, hear it in your voice, when you talk about her. You," she said with a grin, "just have to admit when I'm right and you're wrong. Don't worry, you'll get there."

He arched a brow. "Sarcasm, too?"

"Some. But I don't think I'm wrong this time, either. Do you?"

"I don't know. That's my point." Running his hand over his eyes, he frowned. "Love. I haven't known this woman long enough to be in love. Have I?"

"Huh. How long did you know Christy before you—"

"Shh, you." Days. Mere days after meeting Christy and he knew. Then, he hadn't doubted that instinct, the surety or the strength of what he felt. "Doesn't matter. Meredith isn't Christy, and I'm a different man today than I was then. I don't really know her, Fi."

"Gee, let me think how you could fix that. Hmm. Oh, I know! Perhaps, rather than standing around in my kitchen, you should be with her? Talking to her instead of me? Getting to know her?" His sister gave him a sugary sweet smile brimming with innocence.

He wasn't fooled. Oh, she was concerned, and she certainly could be one of the sweetest women on the planet, but she was also enjoying his torment. That sibling thing. More than that, though. She hated him being alone so often. Worried about him far too much. "What do you think?" she teased.

"I sort of reached that decision on my way here, actually."

"Guess you needed some reinforcement?"

"Guess so."

"Well, you have it." She gave him a tight hug. "Go on now, say goodbye to your niece and follow your heart. Try not to let your shields get in the way."

Yeah. That was always the problem, wasn't it? His damn shields.

He nodded, started to walk away when a thought occurred. What had Meredith asked him for their last day together, when they were going to build a snowman? Oh, right. Turning on his heel, he said, "You wouldn't happen to have any carrots, buttons and…ah, coal?"

"I have those," Fiona said after a moment's pause. "But I don't have a corncob pipe."

"Why would I need a corncob pipe?" Then, shaking his head, he said, "Doesn't matter. Don't need a pipe. Just the other stuff. And maybe an extra scarf if you have one."

She had that, too.

The doorbell rang just as Meredith disconnected the call to her former employer. She'd asked for a reference letter, as she had an interview later that week with one of the city's larger real estate firms. The position was only partially described as a stager, and she didn't yet know what the rest of the responsibilities were, but she felt confident that she'd be offered the job.

She just wished she'd thought of requesting the reference letter sooner. Easy to understand why it had slipped her mind, with it being so occupied by a missing mountain man.

The Get a New Life to-do list seemed a mile long, but retaining a job with dependable income had to come before locating an apartment or returning to San Francisco to pack her belongings. If she couldn't find a job, she couldn't stay. No matter how much she wanted to.

A knock on her bedroom door, followed by someone cracking it open, diverted her attention. It was Rachel. "Meredith?" she said. "Liam is here at the door, asking for you. He has those dogs with him, too! And oh, my, they are gorgeous animals."

Lightning fast, all thoughts of a job and a place to live evaporated, and Meredith's heart went into overdrive. "Yes. Yes, they are beautiful animals." Oh, Lord, was this it? Had he realized…did he miss her…did he want what she did? Pressing her hands down her jeans, she said, "How do I look? Should I change or…?"

"Um. You look gorgeous, just like always." Blue eyes narrowed and then widened in understanding. "Oh! It's that way, is it? You should've told me!"

"I was going to. Eventually. I…well, there might not be anything to tell." Shivers of apprehension whisked along Meredith's skin, bringing about a multitude of goose bumps. "But he's here. And he didn't call or text or…he's here. With the dogs. So, that seems good, doesn't it?"

"I don't know the story," Rachel said, laughing, "so I can't really comment. But when a handsome man shows up unexpectedly, well…I'd say the possibility of good is right up there."

Rachel was right. Liam's presence here had to mean something good, otherwise, why bother with any type of a visit? She hadn't left any of her belongings—mostly because she hadn't had hardly anything with her—at his place. They'd had that amazing conversation on the drive over and they'd said their goodbyes. There wasn't any reason for him to be here.

So, something good.

The thought—that freaking hope—settled her brewing emotions enough that she was able to force her legs to move. She left the bedroom and walked the short distance to the living room, to the front door, opened it and…there they were.

Her guardian angels and the man she hadn't been able to stop thinking about, on Rachel's front porch, looking to Meredith like a dream—her dream—come to life. A flurry of anticipation and hope swam in her stomach.

Both of which she immediately tempered and reminded herself to keep her head out of the clouds. This man might want nothing more than to check in, make sure she was okay.

"Well, hi there," she said, managing to keep her voice level and smooth, as she joined them on the porch. The second she did, the dogs were butting their bodies against her legs, pushing their heads against her hands. Dropping to one knee, she accepted their kisses and scratched behind their ears. "I missed you guys, too!"

Another few minutes of this went on while Liam, who looked as if he hadn't slept in days but somehow retained that rugged sexiness he so effortlessly carried around with him, stood by and watched with a stern expression. Almost as if he were…not angry, exactly, but upset in some form or fashion. So, maybe this wasn't good after all?

Only one way to find out and stop her brain's incessant spinning.

Standing, she leaned against one of the porch's rails for stability, firmed her shoulders and settled her gaze on Liam's. There it was, that sizzle of electricity, that punch of recognition that she'd felt from the very instant she'd first looked into his eyes.

Unfair, really. Glorious, though.

"Hey, Goldi," he said, his voice sounding almost as tired as he looked.

"Hey, back." They stood there quietly, their gazes locked for a few seconds that could've just as easily been a year. "What brings you this way?" she asked, trying to sound natural and not as if her knees were less than ten seconds from buckling. "Everything okay?"

"Yup. Everything is fine." Shoving his hands into the pockets of his coat, he leaned against the porch rail near the steps. "Had lunch with my sister and niece. They live fairly close by. Just figured I'd stop by and see how you were doing. Plus, I…ah…the dogs missed you."

"I missed…them." She was going to leave it at that, but to hell with it. "I missed you, too. And you look tired. Been working a lot?"

"Well, you know, there's all that wizarding that requires my attention."

"Yeah? Saving the world or causing chaos?"

The corners of his lips curled into a grin, wiping away that stern expression. Good. She adored seeing his smile. "Maybe a little of both. And yes, Goldi, I missed you, too."

"Did you now?"

"I just said that, didn't I?"

She laughed. She couldn't help it. "Don't be a grump. I'm glad to see you."

"Feel like seeing me for the rest of the afternoon?"

Happiness bounced through her like a kid's rubber

ball, and it took all of her willpower not to jump up and down and clap her hands. "Depends," she said, modulating her voice to hide her extreme joy. "What do you have in mind? I mean, a girl's gotta be a little choosy in how she devotes an entire afternoon. You only get so many of them, you know."

Green eyes narrowed, and those lips of his? They widened into a bona fide smile. "Well now, I have something in mind, but I'd prefer it be a surprise. What do you think, Goldi? Can you put yourself in my care for a few hours without knowing the details?"

"Sure. I think I can trust you for a few hours at least." Or the rest of her life.

"Excellent." He looked her over from head to toe. "We'll be outside, so you need a coat and gloves. Actual gloves, Goldi, and not just a pair of socks slipped over your hands."

Tipping her chin, she shrugged. "Those socks worked well enough, didn't they?"

"That they did." Another long, searching look that sent her head spinning even more. She'd be lucky to get through the next several hours standing if he kept looking at her that way. Though, maybe that wouldn't be so bad. Considering what happened the last time she couldn't stay on her feet. And then, as if he knew exactly what she was thinking, he did that headshake thing and said, "You're dangerous. Entirely too much so."

"I think you're the dangerous one. Or maybe neither of us is dangerous," she said, once again deciding to just freaking speak her mind. "Maybe there's something else going on here."

He didn't speak; she didn't, either. Max went to Liam and braced his body against him, as if offering support.

And Maggie did the same with Meredith. These dogs. Too smart for their own good.

The air between Liam and Meredith thickened somehow, as if all the unsaid words weighed it down.

Finally, Liam pushed himself off the rail, saying, "Get your coat and such, Goldi. We'll…ah…be waiting in the truck."

She might have nodded, but she couldn't swear to that fact. But she also didn't move from her position until Liam and the dogs had reached his truck, her eyes glued to him, his long-legged walk, the confident manner in which he carried himself.

She loved him. Without doubt, now that she'd seen him again, heard that voice again, looked into those eyes again. And she did not care how illogical or improbable or even impossible the realization. She *knew*. Love existed.

How far that love would take her, how much it would grow and deepen, remained unknown. But it was there for this man, and she saw no reason to deny that truth.

"Why are you still standing there?" Liam hollered, waking her from her trance. "I have plans for you, woman. Don't make me wait all day."

"Don't you call me woman!" she hollered back. "I have a name, you know."

"*Meredith*," he said, "will you please get moving, so we can commence with the afternoon I have planned? I would be ever so grateful."

She laughed. Loudly. And turned on her heel to get her coat and gloves. He had plans. For her. And didn't that sound so very pleasant? Not to mention…intriguing and hopeful and just breathtaking with all the possibilities? Lord. There were *so many* possibilities.

So many possible paths. Some included Liam, some

didn't. And she did not know what he had in mind for the day, or if this was the start of a new path, one that would extend beyond a couple of hours on a Sunday afternoon.

But he was here. He wanted to see *her*. Had admitted to missing her! Right now, those three facts were glorious enough. Miraculous enough.

And the rest? Whatever loomed, she'd take it and run. One second, one minute, one afternoon at a time. Because that was life. *This* was life. She refused to waste any of it.

For the first time in a full friggin' month, Liam's heart didn't ache with emptiness. His head wasn't overflowing with annoying, complex questions he did not want to answer. Wasn't ready to answer. And damn it, the way this woman made him smile.

His cheeks hurt from the strain. Which was both annoying and wonderful. Astounding and irritating. Why did anyone need to smile so much their cheeks hurt?

He did not know, but all in all, he felt better than he had since that afternoon he'd dropped off Meredith. With her, he was…what? Restored? Ridiculous thought, but one he could no longer discount or ignore. Hell, even his bones felt sturdier.

Which seemed to state that Fiona's take on the matter might hold water.

He might be falling in love with Meredith—because he wasn't ready to fully admit he was already there—and if so, he was just going to have to decide what to do about it. Embrace and accept and move forward or tuck his tail between his legs and run away. Pretend and hide.

Sighing, he set the mess aside and decided to just sink himself into the day, into this time with Meredith and let the rest sort itself out as needed. Right now, he was restored. He'd admitted it. More than enough reality for a man like him to absorb at once.

He took her to a local park, showed her the bag of snowman accoutrements he'd gotten from Fiona and told her they were finally going to build that snowman, but that she would have to instruct him on the proper method. Since, yup, he did not have that experience.

Damn it, the smile that wreathed her face made his smile even larger. Made his cheeks hurt even more. The whole world brought into focus by a woman's smile. And he found he…liked that feeling. That realization. Almost as much as—

"No! Liam, you're making his head too big," Meredith said, interrupting his thoughts. Delusions? Maybe that, too. "Now you have to start over."

Cheeks pink from the cold, lips, too, and her hair a disarray of golden curls that all but glittered in the late afternoon sun. Beautiful. Spunky. A pain in the ass.

"I'll have you know that this ball is the perfect size for our snowman's head," he said, wanting to rile her up a bit more. For no other reason than it was fun. "Besides which, what's wrong with having a big head? You've seemed to get along just fine and—"

An icy cold splash of snow hit his face. "I'll have you know that my head is perfectly proportioned to the rest of my body," she said, as she lobbed another snowball his way. This time, he saw it coming and got out of the way. "Now, your head? That's a different story."

Another smile. Another laugh. Another half dozen snowballs before they got back to the question of the correct size for a snowman's head. He gave in. Because doing so made her laugh, tease and smile all that much harder. Good stuff, in Liam's opinion.

"There, look at that," Meredith said, moving to stand

beside him when the snowman was featureless but built. She handed him the bag from Fiona's. "Go on. Give him his personality. His eyes and nose and mouth. Bring him to life, Liam. And then…give him a name. Because every snowman needs a name."

Bring him to life? Like she had done with him?

Asinine thought, so he put it out of his normal-sized head as fast as it had arrived. That thought was for later, when she wasn't in his immediate area messing with his logic.

"Sure. I can do that. Let's see, where to start." He fished through the bag and laid the carrot, buttons and chunks of coal on the snow in front of his creation. And he decided to rile her up a bit more.

Because…why not?

So, while she played with Max and Maggie—tossing them snowballs to leap after—he used the buttons for the eyes and nose, the coal in a nice, even row down the body and then he took that carrot and pressed it flat into the snowman's head for his mouth, instead of sticking out straight for the nose.

She hadn't noticed yet, as she was too busy with the dogs, so he finished by wrapping the scarf around the arms—two tree branches they'd found—instead of circling what would be the snowman's neck.

"There. All done. I now have the experience of building a snowman," he said to Meredith. "And I name him Oliver. Because…well, he looks like an Oliver, don't you think?"

She stopped playing with the dogs to give Oliver the proper amount of attention, and yup, she laughed. Walked to the snowman and gave him another long look. "I have never seen a carrot smile before," she said. "But you know what? He's perfect. Because you made him."

Well, his plan to rile her up had failed. He didn't mind. Not with that smile.

"I like him, too," Liam said. "Thank you. I can now say my life is complete."

Large blue eyes blinked once. Twice. Three times. "Well, every person should build a snowman at least once in their life. So, you're welcome. Thank you for bringing me here, for letting me do this with you. I…I don't know, Liam. You have a way about you."

"So do you," he said, wanting nothing more than to grab her in his arms and kiss her. Long and hard. Soft, too. The want to taste her again wove in next, to claim her as his, to give himself to her and just let the dice fall wherever they landed. *Not yet.* Maybe not ever.

But he might be able to…

Before he could swallow the need that suddenly came over him, wiping out even the desperate want to kiss her, he held out his hand. "Come with me," he said. "I want to talk for a while. I want to share something with you, and I'll warn you. It isn't an easy story."

Curiosity along with a good dose of surprise flashed over her expression, but she nodded. Held out her glove-covered hand to his, and he clasped it tightly. "Whatever you want to talk about, I'm happy to listen. Anything, Liam."

"Oh, I know how you like to talk," he teased. The moment didn't lighten as he'd hoped, but that was okay. It wasn't going to be a light conversation.

He led her to a park bench, where they sat side by side. And then, before he could change his mind or allow the million reasons—*valid* reasons, damn it—why he shouldn't let this woman in any more than he already had, he just pushed out the first sentence. "I am a widower, Meredith. Going on ten years now."

"Oh." Her grip tightened on his, and a bolt of courage, strength, existed there. Comfort. Desire. Acceptance. So much he felt from this woman. So much he felt *for* her. Too much, really. Too fast and too furious. "What was her name?"

"Christy." And then bit by bit, word by word, the story fell from his lips. As if it had just been sitting there, waiting for all this time for Meredith to hear.

He spoke of how they met—via a mutual friend—their courtship, their spur-of-the-moment decision to get married and how they didn't tell anyone until after the fact. Her pregnancy. His assignment. And the horrible tragedy that stole his wife and child while he was photographing birds in the Amazon Basin.

As he spoke the words he never really had before, she listened in silence. She never let go of his hand. She didn't interrupt with questions or her sorrow. She just let him talk.

And oh, he talked for a while. Longer than he'd expected to when he began. Longer than he thought he had it in him to talk about anything, let alone the greatest pain of his life. It was hard, but it wasn't. It was sad, but it was also…freeing in a way he hadn't imagined.

"Remember that picture of the birds? In my office?" he asked when he was done with the rest. "I took that the day before they died, and I remember…I remember thinking that those birds were like Christy and I with our baby on the way. That they represented our life. Happy and bright and colorful, full of song and…hope. So much hope. And I couldn't wait to get back to her, to be there with her, to start our journey as a family."

He heard a deep intake of breath, and her hand tightened another degree. She got it. He didn't have to say anything more. She understood.

But in a way that he couldn't understand, he also felt as if the burden of this pain, this loss, was now halved. As if Meredith had taken on some of the burden for him and was now helping him carry it.

Ludicrous thought, but it fit. It…yeah, it fit.

A hard, almost desperate shudder rolled through his body from head to toe, and she just kept holding on to his hand. Following the shudder, after years of existing without oxygen, of feeling as if the wind had been permanently knocked out of him, he took the first real and true breath he'd inhaled since the moment he'd learned of Christy and his unborn child's fate.

He breathed in as long and deeply as he could. Even then, Meredith didn't talk. But she leaned over to put her head on his shoulder.

The soft brush of her hair smelled like honey and almonds and…home. Lord help him, everything about her resonated as *home*. He supposed he'd have to layer in that realization with the rest, see where it brought him. Form some decisions.

But not now. Perhaps not for a while. He just didn't know. Time was called for.

They sat there for a while longer. The dogs, spent from their boisterous play, were resting on the ground in front of them. Again, there was serenity and peace and a sense of…rejuvenation? Maybe that.

"You're something special, Meredith," Liam finally said. "My dogs knew that about you instantly, and I wasn't too far behind. I…thank you for listening. For sitting with me in that memory and for allowing me to… well, just talk it out, I guess. I'm not used to doing that."

"I know you're not, and Liam? You're welcome." She

kissed him softly and quickly on his cheek. "I'm always here for you. That is something you should know."

And that was it. All that needed to be said. For now anyway.

Chapter Eleven

The interview went well. So well, that Meredith expected to hear good news within the next day or so. Once she did, assuming she did, she could go about checking off the rest of the items on her to-do list. An apartment here in Steamboat Springs. Returning to San Francisco to pack up her belongings and officially move her life here. And she couldn't wait.

Today, though, she had more important matters on her mind. Her period was late. By one full week and that had never happened before.

Never.

So, while she tried to convince herself that she was likely worrying for nothing, that stress and the accident and everything else that had occurred could be more than enough to mess with her body…she *knew*.

And she was petrified.

The second she left the interview, in her second rented

car that matched her first, she drove to a local convenience store and bought two pregnancy tests. Two. So she could verify the results of the first, because yeah, she'd have to for her peace of mind.

And then she'd returned to Rachel's, relieved to find the house empty, and tore open both boxes. Read the instructions. Locked herself in the bathroom and…peed on the first stick.

She waited with her forehead pressed to her knees, forcing air in and out of her lungs. Trying to ignore the panic brewing in her blood. She couldn't be pregnant. She had zero symptoms: no morning sickness and her breasts weren't sore or swollen. Her body felt completely normal, just as it always had. She *couldn't* be pregnant.

She wasn't ready.

Not when everything in her life was finally starting to come together and feel right. Not when everything with Liam was starting to come together and feel real and possible more than blindly and illogically hopeful. Just not now. This wasn't the time. For her, for him, for them.

And oh, God, not after learning about his heartbreaking, tremendous loss.

A wife he'd loved. A baby on the way. Both gone in the blink of an eye, and a man who had already suffered great loss in his lifetime—his parents' deaths and all that missing time with his sister—had to prevail over another loss. It wasn't fair. It made her problems even less important, almost ridiculous, because she'd never had to sustain anything like Liam had.

Enough time had passed to look at the stick. To see if a plus sign or a negative sign had appeared.

But she didn't want to. In this second, she could remain clueless and hang on to her hope that she wasn't—couldn't be—carrying Liam's baby. Her baby. Their baby.

Because it wasn't time for either of them. What would she do? What would he do?

Think this through.

Right. Follow the possible paths. Determine the likeliest scenarios. Put some weight behind the what-if to bolster her courage and remind her that she could handle whatever came her way.

She'd survived getting lost in the mountains during a freak snowstorm, hadn't she? Yes. Okay, so that was nothing compared to the possibility of being pregnant, becoming a mother and raising a child. Even so, it showed she was tenacious. Strong. Capable.

So, she didn't lift her head from her knees. She forced the brewing panic to calm. If a plus sign existed when she looked, then what?

Well, the first thing would be to process the information. Second would be, naturally, telling Liam, because he deserved to know as soon as possible. A difficult, emotional conversation would likely follow. But how would he react? Shock would come first, no doubt. Anger? No. Liam wouldn't be angry, he'd be…scared? Probably even more frightened than she was at this moment, but he wouldn't admit that to himself, let alone to her.

Shocked. Scared. What else? Protective? Based on everything she knew about him, how he'd been with her, then yes…protective. Accountable, too. He wouldn't run from the financial responsibility or the hands-on day in and day out of being a father. She *knew* this. He might attempt to corral the situation into a neat little box so that he felt it was under control. Doable.

What would that mean? A shotgun wedding? Meredith sighed. Yeah, he very well could suggest they marry for the best interests of the baby. And as much as she yearned for…well, everything with this man, she wouldn't settle into a marriage of obligation. That was *not* the life she wanted.

For herself or for Liam.

Of course, if they were to arrive at that beautiful place from her dream where they truly loved each other, couldn't imagine a life without the other…that was an entirely different story. But they weren't there yet. Whether or not she was pregnant.

Breathing deeply, Meredith considered the least likely alternative: that she was wrong and that Liam would run from her, the baby and the responsibility.

No. That was not the man she knew, but…she had to follow through with the thought. For her sake. If the impossible were to happen, what would she do?

Well. Pretty much what she was already doing: creating a life of her own making. The same necessities existed: a job she enjoyed that paid what she needed. A safe home. Friends. Family. Laughter and love and more happiness than sadness.

Yes. The very same framework for a life she had already started to create. That life would simply include one extra person; her son or daughter.

Meredith's panic didn't fully disappear, but the smog in her head cleared. Her heart didn't beat quite so hard, and the nausea swirling in her stomach eased.

If she were indeed pregnant, she'd handle whatever came next. With Liam by her side, in the multiple ways that could occur, or without Liam anywhere to be seen. *She* could do this. On her own, if necessary.

Another deep inhale of oxygen and Meredith lifted her head from her knees, closed her eyes and reached for the pregnancy test she'd left on the edge of the bathtub.

Gripping her hand tightly around the test, she counted to three and opened her eyes.

A bold pink positive sign. She was having Liam's baby.

Whistling to the dogs, Liam tossed the last of his bags into the back of the truck. He'd been offered a last-minute, ten-day assignment in the Australian Outback due to another photographer cancelling because of a family emergency. Liam had almost declined but decided it would do him good on a lot of different levels to get away. So, he accepted.

He needed to think. He needed to separate his emotions from the almighty logic and find a balance. And he needed to do that somewhere else. Somewhere far enough away from Goldi that he couldn't be tempted to jump in up to his eyeballs before he was ready.

And he was *not* ready.

That being said, he couldn't leave the country without seeing her and letting her know where he'd be, how long he'd be gone. That felt necessary. And he wanted to do so in person, not via a text message or a phone call. Which meant he had to get moving as he was flying out of Denver early that evening. He had to drop off Max and Maggie at Fiona's, stop by Rachel's to talk with Meredith and then make the three-ish hour drive to Denver.

At the sound of Liam's whistle, the dogs emerged from the trees, bounding toward him at full speed in all their canine grace.

Ever since the snowman day, when Liam had split open his soul and began to breathe again, Max and Maggie had been more themselves. They hadn't stopped staring and whining at the sofa each night, though, as if hoping Goldi would appear in a flash of smoke.

There were too many nights he'd wished the same.

Just as the dogs swarmed around his feet, the sound of a car driving into his long, twisty driveway pulled his attention. Only took a second to see it was the woman herself, Meredith.

Pride hit him first, that she'd found her way here without trouble. Happiness came next, because she was here on her own accord. Curiosity as to *why* filtered into the mix, followed quickly by the resurgence of his shields.

Oh, they weren't nearly as strong. But they were there. Still. And he couldn't decide if that was good or bad. Worthwhile or…useless. Protective or restrictive.

As she stepped from the car—another rental, he assumed—he was struck by her beauty all over again. She had her long, curly hair swept back in a clip of some sort, but the sides hung loose around her shoulders like a shimmering cloud. A small, tentative smile curved her mouth and she raised one hand in an equally hesitant wave.

Something was wrong.

Apprehension tightened his gut, rippled through his muscles. She walked toward him and he noticed the slight tremble in her chin and the way she worried her bottom lip with her teeth. Her skin, normally pale, appeared about as fragile as a sheet of tissue paper.

Yup, something was wrong. And that realization, the many possibilities of what *could be wrong*, ignited that natural need he had to protect this woman. Right alongside that need, however, existed fear.

Crippling, debilitating fear.

He didn't want to admit the fear. Didn't want to face it, either. So, he did the next best thing and set it aside, like a cup of forgotten coffee that had grown cold. It would be there later, to look at, analyze, consider. Decide how to better manage it or expunge it once and for all.

"Liam," Meredith said when she reached him. Max and Maggie, upon seeing her, had jumped back out of the car and were begging her for attention. Her smile widened at their boisterous, adoring affection. She petted their heads, scratched behind their ears, murmured her hellos. Then, lifting her eyes to Liam's, she let out a breath. "I...hope this isn't a bad time?"

"Never a bad time for you." Whoa. Where had those words, that sentiment, come from? They were true, he realized, despite his fear. He'd always welcome Meredith. *Always.* "I was actually going to stop by and see you, after I dropped off the dogs at Fiona's."

"You were? Drop off the dogs?"

"I was. I'm...heading out on assignment. Australia. I'll be back in a couple of weeks." He resisted the temptation to pull her into his arms and promise her that everything would be okay. He didn't know that anything was wrong, for one thing. For another, he didn't know if that was a promise he could keep. "So, I'm glad you caught me. We could've missed each other."

"Oh. I didn't know...but of course I wouldn't. Why would I?" Rubbing her hands together, she darted her gaze away from his. "Maybe this isn't the best time, then. We can always talk when you get back, and...yeah, that's probably what we should do."

She turned, ready to leave, and while he couldn't define how he knew, he was certain that letting her walk away would prove to be a horrible mistake. "Stop, Meredith." She faced him again. "You came here for a reason, and I have time for you, time for a conversation."

"You're sure?"

Yes. Something was wrong. "Wouldn't have said so if I wasn't."

"Well. I don't know. This conversation shouldn't be rushed. It's important. And…"

Her voice trailed away into nothingness. What was going on here? What thoughts, concerns, fears were swirling in *her* brain? He wished for the ability to take everything negative away from this woman and fill her with nothing but the positive. Let the sunshine wipe out the gloom. "We won't be rushed. I can always change my flight, if necessary. Let's go inside."

For about fifteen seconds, she didn't respond, just stood there with her back straight, looking over his shoulder into the distance. She nodded, pushed her hands into her coat pockets and said, "Yes. You're right. This…is important and it shouldn't wait."

They walked toward the house and Liam's brain went into overdrive. What could be wrong? What might they have to talk about? Was she leaving, going back home to San Francisco? He didn't like the idea of that at all. He wasn't ready to move forward, but he wasn't ready to say goodbye, either. Which meant…he couldn't do anything.

Even if she told him she'd decided to leave.

Less than an hour ago, he'd prepared the house for a two-week absence, and when he'd locked the front door, he certainly didn't know he'd be returning within fifteen minutes. And he couldn't have known that Meredith would be with him, following him inside. Whatever she needed to say, whatever the reason behind this visit, he had the sense that nothing would ever be the same again. That whatever she was about to tell him would change him. Forever.

For the good? For the bad? Yet another question he couldn't answer.

Once inside, Liam nodded toward the sofa, which would now and always be hers. If she was leaving…if he didn't have the necessary time to figure out what he wanted, how to move forward, if he *wanted* to move forward, he would have to replace this couch.

Or not. Hell.

She sat. He did, too, right next to her. Possibly a bad idea, but he had to be near her in case whatever she told him required his comfort. He needed to be close in order to hold her hand or put his arm around her or...well, offer his support. That was true, would always be true, regardless of the fear that seemed prepped and ready to consume him, from the inside out.

"Talk to me, Goldi," he said. "What brought you here today?"

Long lashes dipped in a blink, then another. She cleared her throat and fidgeted in place while a tremble visibly rolled through her slight frame. "I've tried to think of the best way to tell you this. All the way here, I rehearsed how to say what I need to say, but...I don't know if there is a right way. I don't know which words are best or which order to put them in. And...and I almost turned around at least a half dozen times. Because—"

She stopped speaking, shook her head and inhaled another deep, fortifying breath. Blue eyes glistened with the threat of tears, and Lord, all he wanted was to see her smile. Hear her laugh. Let her know that no matter what battles she faced, he'd stand next to her, sword raised, ready to protect and defend and keep her...whole. Safe. Again, words he couldn't say. Wouldn't say until he *knew* he was ready for this, for her and that he could give her all she deserved.

"Tell me, Goldi. Please?"

Yet another breath, deeper than the last. More fluttering of her eyelashes as she blinked. A firm nod. Shoulders straight, jaw set, she reached for his hand.

He held it tightly and with his other hand, tipped her chin so they were eye-to-eye. "Don't you know that you can tell me anything? I'll listen. Whatever it is, you have nothing to be afraid of."

Those words? True. Heartfelt. Real.

Naturally, none of the truth there altered his own fear. His own inabilities. His desperate desire to remain unscathed for the remainder of his life, to never again face excruciating loss. He'd barely survived the first time—with his parents, and hell, he still couldn't figure out if he'd survived, as in *really survived*, losing Christy. All these years, all this time, all his solitude and refusal to become close to anyone and really…how many steps had he traveled?

He couldn't answer that. Not now. Not when this woman stared at him with shiny tear-filled blue eyes and glimmering cloud-like hair. Not when her body shook with shivers. And certainly not when he felt her confusion and fear as if it were his own.

"I'm pregnant, Liam."

That was it, all she said, three little words that held the force of a tsunami. Three little words that sucked every bit of oxygen from his body. Three words. Just three. Yet they changed…everything.

"I'm sorry," he said, feeding the all-consuming need to be absolutely sure he'd heard her correctly. "What did you say?"

More blinks. More breaths. More trembles. "I said that I'm pregnant. I…I found out earlier and…you needed to know right away. I wouldn't keep something like that from you. So, here I am and I know…I know what a shock this is and I—"

She broke off, waiting for him to offer…what? Reassurances, probably, to promise her that he was fine. That she had nothing to worry about. That she wasn't in this alone. And of course, she wasn't. Of course.

But he couldn't breathe. Couldn't think. Damn it, why couldn't he think? She was pregnant. A baby—*his* baby—was even now growing inside of her, and that baby would require the world. Deserved everything he could offer and more.

"You're pregnant?" He'd heard it twice. Why'd he have to hear it a third time?

"Yes. And yes, I am sure. And—" here, her voice strengthened, grew in confidence, and even in the storm of his emotions, he was proud of her "—yes, the baby is yours."

Well, he knew that. Didn't need that fact confirmed, but he understood why she'd put that out there.

No doubts. She didn't want him to worry or question, and he didn't. Wouldn't, with Goldi. But with that unnecessary confirmation, the smallest kernel of joy appeared in the center of the chaos. *Joy.* It was there. He felt it. And damn it all again, that joy increased his fear.

Joy was dangerous. It needed hope to exist, to flourish. And hope…well, he hadn't had a whole lot of luck with hope. Hope, he'd learned, was treacherous. Could make you believe the world was yours for the taking and then suck you down into the pits of hell. In less than a second, without warning. Did he have it in him to hope again? To let that joy flourish and take root?

He did not know.

"Liam? Say something," Meredith said, her voice a tangle of want. "Anything. I don't care what, but you have to say something. Don't let me sit here in this alone."

"You're not alone." The words flew from his throat, his heart and his soul effortlessly. And he meant them completely, but his voice sounded flat and without warmth. He heard it, so yeah, she had.

He tried harder with, "You are never alone, Goldi. I'm sorry for... I just need a minute to catch up, to let this news sink in. But I'm here with you, and this baby will have everything he or she needs. So will you, as far as that goes. Know that. No matter what else."

She swallowed hard and turned her body away from his. Dropped his hand. "I do know that, Liam. I do. And I'm not asking for anything from you that you don't...or won't...want to give. But you had to know. And...well, I guess now you do. So. Okay. You know."

"I *am* here. I swear to that."

"Okay."

Unsaid words weighted the air, and he fought to find... whatever it was she needed to hear. Fought to be a better man for her, for this child he'd just learned would one day be and, yes, for himself, too. A better man than who he had been. A man who'd lived in seclusion, choosing to separate himself from the world in order to create a structure he could exist in without the possibility of anything real ever happening again.

He wanted real. Yearned for real. But yeah, that want, that hope was treacherous. So, he couldn't find the words, the emotion, the sentiment, the confidence and strength she surely needed from him in this space of time. He didn't know how to breach this gap that had appeared between them.

This woman had popped into his life out of nowhere, and he hadn't yet accepted and embraced that miracle, that *hope*. Moving from that to this so quickly was too much.

Time. He needed that time to process. To put everything into perspective and see if he could allow that kernel of joy to flourish into…well, a life. A full, real life that would include Goldi and a child and…a future he'd long given up on.

No, he didn't have the words or the strength or the courage. He didn't have any of those, and explaining all of that seemed impossible. Instead, he opened his arms and said, "Come here, Goldi. Let me hold you for a minute, because you need to know that I am here with you."

A slight hesitation, a quick breath and then there she was, her head pressed against his shoulder, her honey-and-almond-scented hair tickling his jaw. He brought her to him as tightly, as securely as he could. In those minutes, his world felt…right. Sturdy and secure.

No longer fragmented into pieces. So, whole, he guessed. Real.

"You can count on me," he said into her ear with the only promise he was able to offer in this minute. It wasn't enough. Not nearly enough. But he refused to give her hope he did not yet believe in, so really, all he could do was speak the truth. What he *knew* to be true. "You and the baby will never have to worry. You'll be taken care of. I promise."

"I appreciate that," she said, pulling herself free of his hold. "And I know you're a responsible man, Liam. I didn't expect…well, I didn't expect anything less."

Meaning she had expected more? Or just…hoped? Hell if he knew. But saying words he couldn't back up would only hurt them both, even if they would offer a momentary comfort.

"We'll figure this out," he said. "Soon. I just… I'm sorry. It isn't fair to you, but I need a little time, to think and plan. I'm not running away. I'm here. Please believe that."

Remembering his flight, that he had to take the dogs

to his sister's, he looked at his watch. He had a few minutes before he absolutely had to leave, but he'd give her however much time she needed. He'd cancel the assignment. He'd stay if she asked.

But he wanted to go, wanted to have that time to sink into his work so he could process. Consider the past, the future. What he was capable of offering this woman.

Perhaps that made him awful and selfish, just having that want. Yet another mystery he couldn't solve. It was, he decided, what it was. But yes, if she asked him to stay, he would. Without hesitation.

As she had from the very beginning, she seemed to see straight into his brain and read his thoughts. That still disconcerted him, startled him.

"You probably have to leave soon, right?" she asked, pulling herself up to stand. "I won't keep you any longer, and of course take whatever time you need. I have to process, as well. I just found out a few hours ago, so I'm…thinking, too."

"I can cancel the job," he said. "Just say the word, and I'll do so. Or change my flight until tomorrow, if you want to…have more time to talk right now. Seriously. I will do that."

Bringing her fingers to her temple, she rubbed as if a headache brewed. "No. You have a job, and you should go. A couple of weeks, you said? That will give us both plenty of time to think about this, about what we want to do. So, no, don't cancel. Don't delay your flight."

Silence filled the space between them. Uncomfortable, tense silence.

He should cancel. That should be *his* decision. To show her that he meant what he said, that she wasn't alone. That he would be here, through everything and that he would see to her needs. To their child's needs.

But he couldn't quite find the will to say those words, to follow up on them, so he kept his mouth shut. The selfish side of him wanted to escape. Not forever, just for two weeks.

And the longer he didn't say those words, give that offer, make that decision for them, the more tense and hungry the quiet between them became. It was a monster, that silence, demanding what he *could* give but selfishly did not want to. She would have to ask for him to comply and that…well, that did not seem to be happening.

Both of them. More stubborn than anyone had a right to be.

Sighing, he gave into the selfishness. Knew he'd question that decision every hour for the next two weeks, but even that didn't stop him. He needed the time. Desperately. And he'd have to believe that she would understand and that she spoke the truth, that she needed it just as much. Otherwise, why tell him to go? Why offer those assurances if they weren't heartfelt?

Right. So, yeah, he gave in. "Okay, if you're sure. We'll…plan on talking when I return?"

"Of course." Her modulated tone didn't show whatever she felt, what she might be thinking. And as she spoke, she pivoted her entire body away from him, so she faced the door. She wanted to leave. Was waiting to get the hell out of here, so he could do the same. For him? For her? For both of them? "We'll talk when you return. That… sounds like a doable plan."

"It is the plan. Two weeks, Goldi, and we'll figure this out." He came to her then, started to reach for her but had second thoughts. Now wasn't the time. Even if he ached to hold her again, reassure her, give her the world. "Come on. I'll walk you out."

"Oh. I'm fine. I can find the car." And then, she angled toward him just enough that he could see her face. She smiled, but he could easily see it was forced. "It's right outside in your driveway, remember? No chance I'll get lost. I will even swear that I won't get lost going to Rachel's. So, no worries!"

Her attempt to lighten the moment as they went their separate ways on easier ground didn't go unnoticed. She was something, this woman. In such a moment, she wasn't crying or begging him for so much as a glass of water. She wasn't pushing him to do anything at all.

She was, he realized, trying to remind him that she was independent. That she would be okay on her own, without his help or presence. To give him…what? The freedom of choice?

Probably that. But all at once, his fear altered direction, became even fiercer, and he wondered if she was really saying goodbye. As in, a forever goodbye.

"Goldi?" he asked, hearing the fear that resonated through him mirrored in his voice. "You'll be here, right? When I return? You're not going to disappear on me, are you?"

"Oh. I won't disappear." Another smile, this one less forced. "You'll always be able to find me, Liam. If and when you want. Don't worry about that, either. Okay?"

"Two weeks. I'll see you in two weeks." And then, because he needed to know the *precise* moment he'd see her again, he said, "Two weeks from tomorrow. Meet here around three? That will give me plenty of time to get the dogs and…how does that sound?"

She nodded and started toward the door. Paused. Breathed. And he thought, for barely a second, that she was going to say something else, but in the end, she didn't. Just pushed herself forward and walked away, leaving him alone.

Which was the precise state of being that he'd worked so hard for, had fervently believed he'd wanted and had drowned himself in for going on a decade. Truth was, he'd done just fine in that life, had survived without too much trouble.

But that was before Goldi.

Chapter Twelve

Closing her eyes, Meredith sat on the edge of her bed and waited for the bout of nausea to subside. Within days of learning she was pregnant, the morning sickness had begun with a vengeance, as if her body had patiently waited for her brain to be let in on the secret. She'd already started carrying saltine crackers and peppermints in her purse, because she'd also quickly discovered that "morning" sickness really meant "sick all the darn time, so get used to it."

A lot had happened in the last ten days since she'd told Liam they were having a baby. The job had come through, so she was once again gainfully employed. On her own merits. She had that initial flush of satisfaction, that she'd done what she'd set out to do, proven to herself that she didn't require her father's name or input to locate a good job.

And yes, that had felt empowering. Fulfilling.

In the end, though, she discovered that she'd always known that about herself. Always. Which was yet another powerful realization, though one she wished she'd come to earlier. It might have saved her a lot of angst over the years, that knowing. She knew now, and she supposed that was more than good enough. Better now than later, right?

She didn't start her new job for another ten days, but that worked out just fine. That gave her time to start scouting for an apartment, plan for her return to San Francisco to pack and empty her former apartment and see her family. Make those final amends with her dad.

Tell him and the rest of her family that she was pregnant.

Initially, there would be reservations on her parents' part, she knew. They would want her to move home, so they could take care of all that would need to be taken care of. But no. She'd keep her ground, she'd thank them for their support and she'd return here to her new home. Steamboat Springs, Colorado, where she would raise her child.

With Liam? Well, in one way, yes. He'd be here for their son or daughter, she had zero doubt. But that was it.

All that would exist between them was the shared, unconditional love for the baby they created. There wouldn't be anything more. His walls were too thick, too sturdily built, and the force between them—as strong as it was—wouldn't break through.

The look on his face when she'd told him she was pregnant would forever live in her memory. It was one of intense pain. Loss. And in that moment, she understood more about the man than she ever had before. Somewhere in that amazing heart of his, he might love her...

or have the stirrings of love, the beginnings of what she already felt so strongly.

She just didn't think he was ready, would never be able to get himself there, to latch onto that seed and let it grow. Not with the loss he so obviously still fought, existed with, and she couldn't blame him or pretend she knew what that felt like. Walking around, day in and day out, after losing what he had? No. The strength, the courage he'd had to wrap around himself to just breathe was likely more than she'd ever had to gather.

Even more than she'd had to when she was lost and desperate in a storm.

Nothing could compare. And she hoped to God she'd never experience what Liam had, almost as much as she hoped he'd never face anything similar again for the rest of his life.

When she'd left his house that day, the only thought in her mind was to *run*. Far and fast, before the pain of his expression burned into her soul and never let go.

Her heart heavy, she'd driven to Rachel's and considered her options. She wanted to run. Wanted to return to San Francisco and give up on this idea of a life of her own making. Wanted to hide.

By the time she reached Rachel's, however, she knew she'd live up to what she'd told Liam: that she would be here, when he returned, so they could talk. He would always be able to find her, not only because of their child, but because…well, that was how it should be. What was supposed to be. She knew this, even if he didn't. Even if he never reached that conclusion.

As the days continued to pass, the tiny amount of hope that remained drained into nothingness. And oh, she mourned the loss. Not the loss of what could have been, but the loss of what never was…would never be.

The pain on Liam's face, in his eyes, was too deep, too severe for a man to come back from. Her dream was merely that: a dream. A glimpse, she supposed, of what life could be like with the right person, the right type of love, the right foundation.

It just wouldn't be a life she would have with Liam.

But at least she knew what to aim for someday down the road, when the hold Liam had on her heart let go and set her free. Might be years. The baby who grew inside her might very well be married and have a child of their own by the time that occurred. If it ever would.

If it ever could.

He'd be home in just a few days now. She would drive to his house in the mountains, and they would talk.

The conversation would surround the financial responsibilities, she was sure, along with more promises to take care of her, of their child. Maybe they'd discuss if he'd go to obstetrician appointments with her, if he could be there for the birth and if he was thinking far enough ahead, they might delve into how they would parent, visitation, the baby's last name.

Or they might simply sit and look at each other, with that heavy air choking them, so neither could breathe, let alone speak in complete sentences.

One of the two. Or both, in intermittent gaps.

The only rule she had was to tuck her emotions down deep, so they remained under wraps, to remain stoic and logical and keep her focus on the reason for their conversation: the life they were bringing into this world. How they would do that together without being together.

Meredith's hand went to her stomach. *A baby.* Joy existed there, growing inside of her, alive and strong and beautiful.

This was her future. Joy and beauty, and her choice was to revel in that truth, what *would* be, instead of wish for what would never be.

Sweat beaded on the back of Liam's neck. He looked over at the clock, saw that the minutes were ticking away and he wasn't ready yet.

Everything had to be perfect for when Meredith arrived. *He* had to be perfect. So she could see that the time away had done what was needed: gave Liam clarity, allowed him to separate crippling fear from true, unadulterated hope and determine the stronger of the two.

In those first awful days, it seemed that fear would be the champion. Whenever he considered opening his heart more to Meredith, to that life he yearned for, he just couldn't see beyond his past to get to the hope. And hell, the last thing he would ever do was drag Meredith down a path that he couldn't believe in, couldn't be sure he'd be able to travel.

But on day eight, just as he'd reached the decision to remain in his comfortable solitary existence—save for being there for his child, of course—an epiphany had occurred. In the form of three colorful birds, rainbow lorikeets. They were gorgeous creatures, with bright red beaks and exotically hued plumage that included their green wings and tails, blue-to-purple heads and the vivid yellow-orange that circled their necks and dripped down to their breasts.

And just like before, with the paradise tanagers in the Amazon Basin when Christy was pregnant and awaiting his return, these three birds perched on a branch, huddled close together.

A family. Bright and happy and so beautiful to see that it took his breath away. His heart had ramped up to the speed of a runner about to win a marathon, and he waited for these birds to startle and fly off, just as the paradise tanagers had the second he'd snapped their photograph.

But the lorikeets didn't startle or fly off. They watched him boldly, without fear, and remained steadfast on their branch. In their life with each other. As if to state that nothing, not even a man that didn't belong in their world, could chase them off from where they wanted to be, had chosen to be. A grandiose thought, perhaps, but it resonated just the same.

The similarities between the past scene with the paradise tanagers and the present with the rainbow lorikeets were there and couldn't be denied.

Three colorful birds. A branch. That same feeling of belonging together, looking out for one another, as a family should. All that existed, yes, but they were different birds perched on a different branch in a different location.

More than anything else, though, the time was different.

And these birds? They hadn't disappeared in a flutter of wings, rushing off to find a new branch, a *safer* branch to perch on. They'd stayed. They weren't going anywhere.

Silly, probably, that it took three birds to wake Liam the hell up, but wake him up they did.

So very much came into perspective. So very much clicked into place. Obvious conclusions. Most of which he'd known all along but hadn't allowed to gain a foothold.

Christy and Meredith were two different women. The love he felt for Christy was real and solid and would've lasted a lifetime. He was sure of that. They would've been happy. His love for Meredith—because, yes, he did love her, he knew this now without any doubt—was also real and solid and he believed to his soul that it could also last a lifetime.

But different women meant that love altered some, too. It meant the life he would have had with Christy if she hadn't died would also be different than the one he could have with Meredith. Had to be. He had changed. That loss had altered how he viewed pretty much everything. Before, he'd chosen seclusion to shield himself from facing that type of hurt again. Now, due to an epiphany brought on by three steadfast birds, he understood what he hadn't before.

What he most needed to understand.

Yes, losing Christy and his child had given him a front-row view of how precious life was. But rather than hide from more loss, he should be using that awareness to grab on and go for every bit of happiness—of joy— he could. He should be steadfast and sure, refuse to let go and cherish every damn second of good. And hell, Goldi was pure good.

She was light and love and hope. She'd swept in out of nowhere and stolen his heart.

And now she was having his baby. Some would call this a second chance, but Liam…well, again, two different women. Two different lifetimes. Any of the blessings that existed with Meredith weren't his "second chance," they were his *everything*. They were his present. He hoped his future.

Today, he was going to jump in up to his eyeballs and pour himself into that everything. His shields, his want for seclusion, were gone. She might reject him, might reject all he now saw and was ready to grab onto, and yup, that thought rightly scared him. But it was not going to send him running, nor would that possibility change his mind. He was in.

He just hoped she'd listen. Give him a chance. Give them a chance.

The rumble of her car in the driveway brought him to his senses and that sweat on the back of his neck doubled. No, tripled. But that was fine. He *should* be nervous.

This was life. He wanted to feel it all.

When he drove into Steamboat Springs this morning, he'd stopped by the jewelry store before picking up Max and Maggie. Had looked for and chosen a ring. Some would say he was moving too fast, but frankly, he felt as if he'd already waited, had gotten stuck in the mud of his fears, for too damn long. So, yeah, he was set on changing that dynamic.

No more waiting. No more getting stuck.

The ring box was in his pocket. The fire in the fireplace burned softly, gently. His dogs were snoozing by the fire after romping outside for close to an hour. It wasn't the most romantic of scenes, but it was what he had, and he figured Meredith—*Goldi*—would approve. This room was, after all, the very first place they'd ever laid eyes on one another. Seemed fitting.

Hopeful. Possibly joyous.

The knock on the front door came, rousing his dogs, both of whom lifted their heads and looked at Liam in such a way that he would swear they were telling him not to screw this up. That Goldi was theirs, too, and it was about time he brought her home.

"Tell you what, guys," he said. "If I screw this up, you can go with her. I'll visit a lot, don't you worry, but I won't keep her from you. Deal?"

Now the look they gave him could only be described as pity. Max growled low in his throat, and Maggie whined. Well. They didn't like that idea any more than they enjoyed being with him without Goldi. Seemed they wanted it all, just as he did.

"I'll give it my best shot," he said, just as Goldi knocked for the second time. His stomach turned over and his legs held the consistency of a bowl of jelly. Pitiful. But glorious, too, that this woman could do this and so much more to him, for him. He went to the door and after sending a silent prayer upward, opened it. And there she was.

The woman he loved.

"Hey, there," he said, holding the door open wider and doing his level best to ignore the swarming of bees—couldn't be butterflies—in his gut. She wore her hair long and loose, her eyes were bright and that smile…he lived for that smile. "Come on in. I…how was the drive?"

"I didn't get lost, so there's that." She walked in and unzipped her coat, which she handed to him. Her voice, calm and cool and modulated, told him a lot. Told him she was hurting beneath her collected, easy-breezy facade, and he hated that he'd put her in such a place. "How was your trip?" she asked. "Did you get everything you needed?"

"I did. More than I expected." He hung her coat in the closet. "It was the best trip I've had, ever. I…got more than I hoped for. More than I thought possible." And because he did not want her to continue to think he was referring to his job, to the photographs he went to Australia to shoot, he said, "I thought about us. Constantly, Goldi. And…well, I'm so glad you're here."

She blinked. Nodded. "I thought a lot about us, too. Every day."

"Well then, I'd say we each have a lot to talk about."

"Yes. We do." A sigh teased from her lungs, and her shoulders shook just a little. "I'm glad I'm here, too,

Liam. Happy to see you. It seems like I haven't in… forever."

"I know. Me, too." There was so much he needed to say that the words were all but fighting each other to come out. But not yet. Holding out his hand, he waited for her to take hold. When she did, he said, "Come with me. Let's sit down and have that conversation."

They moved into the living room, and he assumed she'd sit on the couch, but she didn't. She didn't sit anywhere, just stood in front of the fire, holding his hand for dear life.

Her chin trembled and she shifted her gaze away from his to stare at the floor. She was nervous. Scared, maybe, of what he would say. And while he'd wanted to ease her into the moment, into sharing all that he saw for them, he now believed that would be a mistake.

She looked like those paradise tanagers. A second away from startling. A second away from flying into the sky and leaving him alone, watching her departure. Wishing she'd return.

And his Goldi wasn't a paradise tanager. She was a rainbow lorikeet, even if she didn't yet know that. So. Whether it was the right time or the wrong time, he let go of her hand to reach into his pocket. Felt for the ring box to assure himself it was still there and then…he threw caution and common sense and logic and every last one of his useless fears into the wind.

And he knelt in front of Goldi. Took her hand again and, ignoring the buzzing bees in his stomach that refused to settle, said, "I meant to do this differently. I meant to explain everything I've realized and why. I meant to turn on some music, so you could hear ABBA. I meant to be…ah…clear and eloquent, maybe a little romantic, but I can't wait."

Those blue eyes of hers narrowed and a shiver, long and loose, ran through her from head to toe. "If you're about to do what I think, then you should probably stop," she said, her words wobbly. "I don't want a marriage of convenience. I don't want you to think you have to marry me out of some form of responsibility, to ease your conscience. I… I…"

Her words disappeared into the air, but she didn't let go and she didn't look away.

That bolstered his hope, despite what she'd said. And of course, she would think that was what this was about. Of course she would. Well, Liam would have to change that mindset.

Pronto. "Close your eyes for me, Goldi, so you can really listen to my voice as I talk," he said, operating on pure instinct. "The first time you heard my voice, your eyes were closed and you had that dream. The one you still haven't told me about, but based on the little you said, I believe it was an incredible dream. About us. Am I correct in that belief?"

Moisture filled her eyes. "Yes. It was incredible and it was about us."

"Okay, then. Close your eyes, darlin', and let me talk. Listen. And see if you can hear the truth in my voice without any other distractions." He paused for a few seconds, mostly to try to find the words he *would* say, now that the moment was here. "Can you do that for me?"

She breathed in and nodded. "I can."

Max and Maggie, who hadn't yet greeted her, padded to her from the fireplace, standing sentry, one on each side. Even in this moment, one with so much riding on the outcome, he was amused by their stance. As much as they were Liam's dogs, Goldi belonged to them.

And they weren't going to let her fall.

Their presence seemed to offer her a sense of comfort. She closed her eyes, he tightened his hold on her hand and while he hadn't yet chosen the exact words to say, he decided to let his emotions lead his tongue. And he started with the most emotional of them all.

"I love you, Goldi. I do. And I have for what feels like forever, for far longer than the actual time we've known each other. So, I can't define when this love began or when it became so big that it could no longer be ignored. I just know, with every bone in my body, that I am in love with you. Completely."

Another breath, this one larger than the last, but she didn't speak. She didn't open her eyes. Just stood there, holding on to him, in…well, trust was there. Belief of some sort. And perhaps she had the same hope he did. He wouldn't know unless he kept talking.

"But see, even though I recognized this fact, that I love you, I wasn't ready to do anything with it, wasn't even ready to admit it to myself. I was edging in the right direction, but I think…no, I know, I would've proceeded slowly. With caution. But I was getting there."

"You started opening up to me, about your life," she said softly, eyes still closed. "So, I thought so. Wondered. But I didn't know for sure. I…just didn't."

"How could you?" His turn to breathe. The bees were still there, but not quite as many and not quite as strong. "When you came here to tell me about the baby, I…and it shames me to admit this, Goldi, but I got scared. Because you were already so important in my life, and you'd already chiseled into my shields. Add in a baby and the past seemed to be repeating itself."

"I get why you were scared. I have been scared, too."

That pained him incredibly, to hear her say this. "I'm sorry, sweetheart. So damn sorry I couldn't see the past from the present, couldn't stop them from merging together. I just didn't have the ability to do so in that moment, but I wish I had. I wish I could go back and—"

"You don't have to apologize," she said quickly, her words running together. "It was a shock for both of us, and you were still good to me, Liam. Still calm and patient. You just weren't ready to dive in deep, and I don't know if I was, either. Not really."

"I'm still sorry. Forgive me?"

"There is nothing to forgive," she said, as stubborn as always. God, he loved that about her, too, that she didn't back down. That she held her ground. "Can I open my eyes yet?"

"Not yet. Soon." Swallowing, he continued the path he'd taken, telling her about the paradise tanager photograph, how when he'd shot it, he'd been filled with happiness for the future he'd surely have with Christy and as a father. He told Meredith what those birds had represented and how they'd flown away almost instantly.

"It was later that day that I found out that Christy had died, and ever since, I've connected that photograph to my future crumbling into dust. To losing what I loved most. That beauty...well, that it doesn't last, I guess."

A sob escaped from between her lips. "I can see how you would make such a comparison. I think I would, too. And, Liam, I am so very sorry. You don't know how—"

"Shh. I'm okay, Goldi. I wasn't, for a long time, but I am now. Thanks to you." Then, before this woman he loved keeled over because he'd made her stand with her eyes closed for minutes on end, he then told her about the rainbow lorikeets, about what had transpired mere days ago. How in that moment, all he'd already known became crystal clear, solidified and sent his fear into the shadows. How hope and joy had done that.

How *she* had done that. For him.

Now came the most important, the most vital, of all he wanted—needed—to say. And Lord, he prayed he got it right. Or close enough to right that it wasn't wrong. He'd take that. He'd count that as a win.

Pulling the ring box from his pocket with his free hand, he said, "You can open your eyes now, but only if you promise not to say a word until I'm finished."

She nodded, said, "I promise," and opened her eyes. Looked down and saw the ring box, which he'd opened, so the diamond solitaire sat front and center. "Liam! I just said—"

"That you promised to let me finish, so let me do so." Another nod, but it came slower. "I love you, Meredith. I do. With my heart and my soul and my brain. I can no longer imagine waking up every day without you beside me or without 'Mamma Mia' playing too loud and you dancing in the kitchen. Or without you kicking my butt in Hedbanz. Or," he said, "though it is difficult to admit this, your incessant questions and love for talking. I can't live…my—"

Here, he broke off as emotion overwhelmed him, caught in his throat and stole the words he needed to say the most. Okay. He could do this. What was the worst that would happen?

She could say no. That was the worst, and he would respect her decision. But he wouldn't give up easily. Couldn't. Not for this woman.

Steadier again, he looked straight into her eyes, cleared his throat and said, "My life doesn't work without you, not how it should. Not the way it is meant to. So, I'm asking you to marry me. Because I can no longer see a life that doesn't include you beside me."

"Liam." She breathed his name more than she said it. "Are you sure?"

"Very sure. And we don't have to marry tomorrow or next week. Or hell," he said, feeling his confidence grow, "next year."

"Next year, huh?" she said, a glimmer of amusement in her voice, her expression. "I don't know about that. Seems a little too undefined for my liking, but Liam, you—"

"I'll marry you tomorrow," he said. "Now, if we could. But I want this to be your choice, when you feel confident that I have your heart and will keep it whole. Forever."

"I love you so much." Tears welled and spilled down her cheeks. "Have for a while now and, yes, I know this about you. You've shown it to me from day one."

"Is that a yes, Goldi?" He knew it was, but he had to hear her say the word. Had to know that she was his, that he was hers, before he could fully welcome the joy and revel in the promise of the life he would have with this woman. "Will you walk with me down this path of ours?"

"Yes, Liam," she said, her voice strong. Sure. Steadfast. "I will walk with you."

And with those words, Liam reached for her left hand and slipped the ring on her finger, sealing the deal.

She was his. He was hers. From this moment forward, he would cherish and treasure his Goldilocks, care for her, raise his sword in defense. And he knew without question that this woman would do the same for him. Each day. Every day.

For the rest of their lives.

Epilogue

Warm, brilliant sun shone down on Meredith's shoulders. Today marked her and Liam's daughter's first full month of life, and they were celebrating with a picnic outside their house. It was Liam's idea, his surprise, and since Teagan, which meant "beautiful," hadn't given them many hours of sleep last night, Meredith had agreed.

Her infant daughter always seemed calmer when they were outside in nature, which seemed to show she took after her father in that regard. In other ways, too. She had Liam's rich, dark hair and green-and-amber eyes. What she had of Meredith's, so far, at least, was a love for ABBA and a very vocal set of lungs. This amused Liam to no end.

He liked to tease Meredith—whom he still called Goldi most of the time—that she'd brought sound back into his life due to her love of talking. She didn't think he'd ever fully understand that her love of talking hadn't existed until she'd met him. It was with Liam that she had truly found her voice, and it was their conversations she loved.

Stretching her legs on the quilt Liam had laid on the ground, Meredith waited for her husband—they'd married when she was six months pregnant—to bring actual food to their picnic and looked over at her sleeping daughter who rested next to her, protected from the sun by the arch of the tree's branches above them.

This tiny baby was…everything. Happiness and love and sweetness all bundled together in one beautiful, if loud, package. And Meredith couldn't wait to see the person her daughter would grow into. What her interests would someday be, what her smile would look like and if she would laugh in Liam's booming or in her mother's softer, yet no less joyous, manner.

The storm that had brought her to this life, to the man she loved, no longer held any remnants of the terror she'd felt that night.

How could it? If not for that storm, she might never have found Liam, never dreamed about the life she now led, never become a mother to Teagan.

Of course, when she said such things to Liam, his logical brain forced him to point out that she wouldn't have known the difference. That she couldn't have missed what she didn't have, hadn't known about. But he was wrong. She would've known in her heart and her soul that her life lacked something. *Someone.* And she would've yearned.

Now, the most she yearned for was more than three hours of sleep at a time, but that, too, would come to her again. Until the next baby and then the next.

Three was the number that she and Liam had agreed upon, but she kind of thought they'd end up with four.

In her dream, they'd only had two children, but…well, dreams could change.

Her husband appeared then with a picnic basket in his hands and Max and Maggie at his heels.

The shepherds came to her first, to show their love, before carefully taking up their guard-dog positions around Teagan, one at her feet and the other above her head. She was theirs, too. One of the pack. And they were never far from the baby for very long.

"Hope you're hungry," Liam said, dropping onto the blanket next to her. "And if so, you better eat up fast. Before the little one decides she's hungrier."

This man treated her so well. Cared for her. Protected her. Allowed her to do the same for him, so what they ended up with was a true give and take. A true partnership.

She was easily the luckiest woman in the world.

"I am hungry," she said. "But first, if you don't mind, I could use a hug. Maybe a kiss."

His arms came around her, his lips met hers and just like their very first kiss, the world disappeared and all that was left was just the two of them. The emotion that existed between them, their friendship and…yes, the heat that erupted into being.

Instantly.

She fell into the kiss, into the man, and could've stayed that way, locked in his embrace, with his mouth on hers, for all eternity. If not for Teagan deciding that now was the precise time to wake up and demand to be fed.

Her whimper turned to a wail, which led the dogs to whining and then howling, which softened Teagan's tears, rather than ramping them up in volume.

Liam broke off the kiss, ran his hand down the side of her face. "I love you, Goldi."

"I love you, too." Meredith turned to reach for the baby. "More than you know, even."

"Oh, I have a good idea. Even so, I am pretty sure I love you more," he teased. "I mean, ABBA. In the morning, afternoon and when I'm trying to work. Just saying."

Shifting Teagan so that she could feed her, Meredith smiled at her husband. He did put up with a lot, especially for a man who had lived in these mountains for so long in almost complete solitude.

"A good point. I can start using my earbuds more often, to give you some peace."

"You could, but that wouldn't be you," he said, playing with Teagan's tiny fingers. "And you are the woman of my dreams. So, don't change. A thing. Okay?"

And that...well, that said it all.

* * * * *

THEIR CHRISTMAS ANGEL,
the next book in Tracy Madison's delightful series,
THE COLORADO FOSTERS,
will be available in November 2017 wherever
Mills & Boon Cherish books and ebooks are sold!
And don't miss out on previous books in the series:
FROM GOOD GUY TO GROOM
ROCK-A-BYE BRIDE
DYLAN'S DADDY DILEMMA
Available now from Cherish!

MILLS & BOON®

Cherish™

EXPERIENCE THE ULTIMATE RUSH OF FALLING IN LOVE

A sneak peek at next month's titles...

In stores from 7th September 2017:

- **Whisked Away by Her Sicilian Boss** – Rebecca Winters *and* **The Maverick's Return** – Marie Ferrarella
- **The Sheikh's Pregnant Bride** – Jessica Gilmore *and* **A Conard County Courtship** – Rachel Lee

In stores from 5th October 2017:

- **A Proposal from the Italian Count** – Lucy Gordon *and* **Garrett Bravo's Runaway Bride** – Christine Rimmer
- **Claiming His Secret Royal Heir** – Nina Milne *and* **Do You Take This Baby?** – Wendy Warren

---

MILLS & BOON®

EXCLUSIVE EXTRACT

Crown Prince Frederick of Lycander needs a wife
and an heir, and discovering he has a secret son with
beautiful supermodel Sunita makes him determined
to claim both!

Read on for a sneak preview of
CLAIMING HIS SECRET HEIR

'You have a baby?'

Frederick's hazel eyes widened in puzzlement, a small
frown creasing his brow as he took another step into her
sanctum. His gaze rested on each and every item of Amil's.

'Yes.' The word was a whisper, all Sunita could
manage as her tummy hollowed and she grasped the
door jamb with lifeless fingers.

'How old?' Each syllable was ice cold, edged with
glass and she nearly flinched. No, she would not be
intimidated. Not here. Not now. What was done was
done, and, rightly or wrongly, she knew if she could
turn back time she would make the same decision.

'Girl or boy?'

'Boy.' Each question, each answer brought them
closer and closer to the inevitable and her brain wouldn't
function. Instead, all she could focus on was his face,
the dawn of emotion – wonder, anger, fear and surely
hope too? That last was so unexpected that it jolted her
into further words. 'His name is Amil.'

'Amil,' he repeated. He took another step forward and instinctively she moved as well, as if to protect the life she had built, putting herself between him and her home. 'Is he mine?'

For an instant it was if the world went out of focus. She could almost see a line being drawn in the sands of time – this was the instant that separated before and after. For one brief instant she nearly took the coward's route, wondered if he would swallow the lie that Amil was Sam's. Then realised she could not, would not do that. 'Yes. He is yours. Amil is your son.'

Now she understood the origins of a deafening silence. This one trolled the room, echoed in her ears until she wanted to shout. Instead she waited, saw his body freeze, saw the gamut of emotion cross his face, watched as it settled into an anger so ice cold a shiver rippled her skin. Panic twisted her insides – the die had been cast and she knew now that whatever happened, life would never be the same.

Don't miss
CLAIMING HIS SECRET HEIR
by Nina Milne

Available October 2017
www.millsandboon.co.uk